Forged in Fire

Forged in Fire

THISTLEMAN THISTLEMASTER

PALMETTO
PUBLISHING
Charleston, SC
www.PalmettoPublishing.com

Copyright © 2024 by Thistleman Thistlemaster

All rights reserved

No portion of this book may be reproduced, stored in a retrieval system, or transmitted in any form by any means—electronic, mechanical, photocopy, recording, or other—except for brief quotations in printed reviews, without prior permission of the author.

Paperback ISBN: 979-8-8229-4230-1

Heaven's Fall
Book 1: Forged in Fire
Table of Contents

Prologue 6
Chapter 1: My First Contract 21
Chapter 2: Kurstwood 38
Chapter 3: Awakening 46
Chapter 4: Versailles 53
Chapter 5: Duke Vermillion 63
Chapter 6: Ambush 74
Chapter 7: Port City of Njord 86
Chapter 8: The Adventurer's Guild Exam 100
Chapter 9: Welcome to the Guild! 108
Chapter 10: The Skeever and the Bear 114
Chapter 11: My First Quest 120
Chapter 12: Of Horror and Hornets 129
Chapter 13 Prize and a Party 138
Chapter 14: A New Normal 147
Chapter 15: An Unlikely Friendship? 153
Chapter 16: The Great House War 159
Chapter 17: Prelude to Disaster 167
Chapter 18: Night of Blood 174
Chapter 19: A Demon's Solution to the Orphan problem 185
Chapter 20: The Art of Darkness 192
Chapter 21: The Hunt Begins 200
Chapter 22: A Painful Lesson 211
Epilogue: The Little She-Devil of Njord 219

Prologue

"TAKE COVER!" Maria bellowed, her party already dashing to join her for cover behind a pile of debris within the streets of the embattled city.

"Blessed is the light which protects us from harm, Divine Shield Wall!" Maria chanted quickly as her melodic song unleashed a wave of golden streams crisscrossing into a barrier behind them.

KRA-KOOM!

The shield went up not a moment too soon; the sonorous impact of steel on stone sent a shockwave of sound roiling through the city streets. A hurricane of concrete chunks tore through the dozens of red-and-black humanoid demons that flooded the road between the party and the extremely out-of-place ruins of an ancient castle.

Countless chunks of debris, black blood, and hunks of viscera collided with the shield wall, sending out white ripples with each impact before being repelled, while the force of the wind danced with Maria's golden locks of hair.

"Gods be praised! I can understand getting the elves and demi-humans together, but it still astounds me that you even brought the giants to our side!" the paladin crowed, even as he looked mournfully at his unused tower shield. "Still... you could have let me block that one."

However, the paladin seemed to have second thoughts as the ground shook under their feet, and a long shadow blocked out the sun.

"*Amplify Voice. Divine Communication.* THANKS FOR THE COVER, BROMI. WATCH OUR BACKS FROM THERE. WE'RE GOING IN!" Maria's voice resonated with a force tenfold as loud as an average man's shout, prompting her party to cover their ears.

The humanoid skyscraper roared in response, rattling the remaining unbroken glass windows with another gust of wind.

"Ssseeee here, you need to warn usss when you're going to do that!" a snake-like hiss escaped from under the hooded wraps of their assassin.

"Ah, sorry Si-Khola. C'mon, we need to hurry! Oh, and Parth... Bromi said your shield ain't shit," Maria jabbed mercilessly, with the sweetest voice and purest expression. To add insult to injury, she knocked twice on Parth's shield before dashing toward the castle.

"Geralt, that means you too! We need you to give us cover fire, and we can't miss our rendezvous!" Maria's words startled the archer from his trance. He looked away from the colossal creature and ran after the group as it charged into a hailstorm of magic and arrows.

"*Amplification. Greater Range. Greater Strength. Hurricane Force. Perfect Strike. Dragon Arrow!*" Geralt grimaced as he layered on a multitude of rapid-cast spells and notched a bolt the size of a javelin onto his great bow. A mana vortex encircled the bolt, which he released with a heavy *twang*.

The bolt shattered all the windows along its path as it soared over the party's heads and blew a hole through a bus-sized demon as it stepped out of the door from the castle. His eyes narrowed uneasily at the supernatural flow of miasma coming from the castle.

"Tch. This is too damn easy."

Tendrils of the murky clouds overflowed from the walls and poured out from the cracks, and yet, for all its show and lack of delivery, he still couldn't shake the dying words of the Plague Demon Lord from his mind.

"Though I have met my end, you shall all still fall! Foolish mortals! We... were all that held back... those monsters... from the wastelands..."

The Demon Lord's dying words and blood-curdling raspy laugh felt almost regretful that he couldn't witness this himself. *So why did it feel so damn easy in comparison? Even his generals put up a better fight than this... I would have expected more from something as insane as a second demon lord's appearance.*

Almost as if to spite and curse his thoughts when they were mere feet from the castle gates, the earth trembled violently beneath them—the crack and roar of shattering stone and breaking concrete rippled through the air.

"THE DAMN HELL IS THAT DAFT GIANT TRYING TO DO NOW?!" Parth howled in rage as he tried to steady himself against the castle walls. Geralt saw the blood drain from Maria's once flush face, her beauty shining through the horror.

Amidst the overwhelming noise of the collapsing skyscrapers, another deafening roar steadily grew as the quake only worsened.

"GET IN THE CASTLE NOW!" Maria shrieked as a plume of lava tore a hole through the earth beneath Bromi's feat. Geralt scrambled to dive into the castle as Maria, Parth, and Si-Khola slammed the doors shut.

Before the doors slammed shut, and through the waves of superheated smoke and debris, Geralt caught a glimpse of a towering nightmare cloaked in bone and flame. He shivered as a single red eye opened from the creature's shoulder and stared straight through his soul, as a sea of lava and melted flesh flowed past the demon's feet.

Nothing could block the deafening cries of pain from the giant, and there was no solace to be had when it finally fell silent.

"The fuck did you say that was?" Geralt cried as they rushed through the silent halls into the inner court of the ruin.

"Again, that *wasn't* the demon lord! Our target is further in, so just keep yourself together!" Maria pressed onward, her voice strained.

"Even if you're the legendary hero, *how would you know that?* Not even the Plague Demon Lord could take out the king of the giants like that!" Geralt nervously twitched, his whining voice shaking as he glanced over his shoulder.

"From my peopless's hisstory, the ancient dragonsssss were once capable of ssssuch featsss." Si-Khola mused back, his snake-like tongue slithering between his wrappings.

"Hmph. And your people's continued reverence of a heretical and extinct race is why we keep hunting you!" Parth exclaimed in self-righteous indignation.

"What do you mean, *you people?* Jussst because we didn't want to join *Ishhtar* in her genocide, you think itss's right to kill usss too?" Si-Khola countered, his black daggers gleaming while his tongue practically flung spittle as he stormed toward Parth.

The *kling* of a cap bouncing across the stone floor snagged their attention, along with a silvery radiance that danced across the floor.

"Through purity, there is peace. Through peace, there is love. From love, there is light. And from light, there is hope. Together, let the light and hope of our souls drive back the darkness! *Heavenly Blessing!*" Maria held the glass bottle and focused on it with absolute zeal. Its contents radiated out and cleansed away the darkness, revealing a malevolent vortex of dark energy hidden in the shadows and purging away the miasma pouring from it.

"Have you calmed yourselves? The void realm lies beyond here... we cannot falter when we face him." Maria glanced back between Parth and Si-Khola, pouting just mildly enough to guilt them.

"Ah, sorry 'bout that mate." Parth's eyes stared downwards shamefully as he dropped his clerical piety and let a hint of his Aussie accent through. He held his hand on Si-Khola's shoulder firmly. "This damn miasma's getting to my head."

"Ahhh, itss's fine. At leassst—"

The reptilian closed his eyes and suddenly dropped to his knees in a reverent bow as waves of golden light flowed into the room from another portal.

"Praise be, the gods have come!" Parth exclaimed in pure, unfiltered joy.

They didn't dare raise their heads, enraptured as they were by a divine voice sweeter than honey.

"You have done well to make it here, your blessing has opened our way. It is as I feared, the nine would never have let you through if they knew we were coming. The fey are barely holding on, and the other armies are collapsing."

"*What?! There are NINE of them?! Why didn't you t—*" Geralt leaped up, eyes wide, staring at the goddess in disbelief.

"Hush child, there is no need to worry. This is the only way, so do not be alarmed." The goddess cradled the man's head between soft white hands as a golden glow poured over his body.

"Ahh, you're right. This is... no time to worry." Geralt smiled, entranced as the goddess stared deeply into his soul through her golden eye, and a stupid smile stretched across his face.

"That's enough chatter, Almalexia. We have work to do, before this rock goes the way of the dragons." A stout god wielding a lightning-clad hammer barreled through the golden portal, his gruff Nordic voice starkly contrasting with Almalexia's enrapturing melody.

"It's the Thunderer himself! And... and...!" the paladin chirped up, the visage of childish excitement and joy in its purest form as if someone had finally met their greatest childhood heroes as more gods and goddesses came through the portal.

"With this... with this we can truly save the world! We can kill the Demon Lord!" Parth exclaimed; in his manic joy, he completely missed the guilt-ridden glance between Maria and Almalexia.

A tyrannical figure rose from behind a large, black granite pedestal interlaced with lines of copper and arcane diagrams.

It was a towering monster, standing taller than two men. It walked around the pedestal, its jet-black gauntlets scraping across the stone as it passed by.

Numerous mana crystals attached to small towers at even junctures around the inner and outer rings of a diagram that spanned the center of the room. Their singular purpose was clear: they gathered a relentless torrent of miasma and dark energy and redirected it into countless mana crystals and mystical towers scattered throughout the expansive lair. Numerous mirrors lined the outer walls, reflecting the faint magical glow emanating from everything in the room.

They reflected various distorted shapes and sizes and enhanced the crimson colors that stained the joints of the monster's armor. A long sharp bone protruded from each arm and curved like a wicked talon.

"It has been… so very long," the monster murmured to itself, its voice barely a low, sonorous growl.

The monster reached up and touched one of the four black horns that grew from his head, slowly feeling how each one curved to one of four points by each corner of his face.

"I wonder… if there are any still left who remember my name?" The creature spoke again as if expecting an answer from the shadows. His yellow eyes narrowed like a predator, hunting through each and every stone.

Scars from ten thousand years of research combed the walls, forged from failed experiments and weapons tests, as well as the extensive patchwork repairs from those that succeeded.

He carried on with his grisly tasks in this mind-numbing eternity, in a prison of his own making.

"Time, time, time… soon, so soon… enough miasma will be ready. It has been long enough."

Sendrien Dagon, the eldest daemon and the First Demon Lord, born in the Age of Dragons and forged in the flames of Ishtar's War of Extermination, heralding the beginning of the Era of the Gods.

In the ages of his self-isolation, his sole focus was on perfecting his weapon of destruction and amassing enough power to guarantee the end of the world.

Consequently, he had become genuinely ignorant of the world at large, himself, and his new station as Demon Lord. The miasma, being gathered and concentrated across millennia, leaked through the gate over time into the world he no longer cared to see. All that was left was the gnawing madness from the God of Darkness.

And it was then that the shadows answered once more.

I clutched my forehead as I heard the endless voices again. Sometimes they were silent, and other times they were sonorous echoes ricocheting throughout my head, but most often, they were soft murmurs crawling through the fabric of my reality.

Eat their hearts. Devour them all. Burn and Dominate.

"Shut up!"

Pillage their lands. Break their spirits.

"SHUT THE FUCK UP!" I screamed in rage as my frustrations boiled over once again. I knew it was pointless, but still...

How long has it been?

It got harder and harder to remember as time passed on... endlessly cycling without any sense of actual day or night. My memories... it felt like they filled with more and more blanks. Time... lost... and yet every time I tried to focus on it...

Claim their souls. Take their lands. Make them bleed.

"Never, ah, it can never just be a moment's peace, can it?"

This damnable voice just won't stop...

Strip the flesh.

It makes it so damn hard to think...

Salt the wounds.

Sometimes I just wanted to scream it in to silence...

Make them suffer.

"SILENCE!" My frustrations boiled over as I bellowed out once more. Or had I? *How many times have I gone through this? At least, it should all be over soon... after ten thousand years everything is finally ready.*

Heed my call.

Yeah, right, as if I will ever accept your command, Shitty God.

Eat their hearts. Devour them all. Burn and Dominate.

Here it goes, on repeat again. This madness just never ends... you just stopped trying after only a few centuries, didn't you?

Pillage their lands. Break their spirits.

God-damned autopilot is what this is...

Claim their souls. Take their lands. Make them bleed.

Hmm? What in the hells wandered in here? Last I checked, this area was uninhabitable when I moved in...

A pair of demons sprinted down the hall, primarily humanoid in shape, with black and red blotched skin. They had a couple of horns atop their head, which had grown to a modest length—nothing compared to mine but respectable enough.

But... weren't they coming from the direction of the portal? They dropped to their knees and lowered their heads as soon as they saw me. They quaked in the presence of their lord, though I did not yet know it was me.

"Master! We are sorry, for we have failed you! The enemy is coming here, they are trying to stop us!"

Who is here? What enemy? Why does anyone know where I am?! And... what strange-looking daemons? Something feels off about them. What strange behavior too... Do they fear me, or is that reverence? Are they really descendants of the daemons I knew?

"Detect Life. Eyes of Magnus." My voice rumbled soft yet deep. A shortened incantation would still be plenty for my purposes, and at my age, I certainly had mana to spare.

A pair of magical eyes opened in the clouds above a city spanning wide across an otherwise barren wasteland.

A suffocating magical aura rained down from the great eyes, and I could feel the endless stream of information of every minute detail as it poured into my mind.

Rocky dunes stretched for miles beyond the city's bounds, and howling winds carried grating sand through the air at speeds that could easily strip the bark from trees. No water… no life… nonetheless, a city was built here with advanced construction techniques, floating defensive platforms, and highways crossing between towers. At least my dilapidated castle stood untouched at the center of it, in stark contrast to the changes that occurred all around it. Needless to say, it was quite shocking.

Since when did a city get built around my castle?! It is overflowing with my miasma, and nothing should be able to survive! Yet these strange daemons are not only living in it… but thriving. How? To top it off… Look at all these other creatures here! Humans, elves, dwarves, goblins, giants, and so many others… all fighting the daemons? They must have come because of these new daemons… but why did those come here in the first place?

I sighed audibly and closed my eyes. I… was tired of it all.

It doesn't matter if they managed to find out what I was up to; it's too late for them. The miasma will be unleashed momentarily. The world will perish, and I, too, will die when the miasma runs its course.

I grimaced for a moment.

But… that doesn't seem right? Why? Ah, it won't do to dwell on the matter. I have work to finish.

My mind felt hazy again. *Broken.*

A pool of viscous black formed in the air next to me, and a blade handle dripped out from its inky depths. I grasped the handle and pulled out the lethal weapon from the darkness. Its brutal design was made for a singular purpose.

Its blade was a foot shy from being as long as the average man, with a snake-like trough running down the center to let the blood flow out when someone was stabbed.

I forged it with adamantium and fused the blade with magecite, the base mineral used to develop mana crystals. A laborious, lengthy, and dangerous process, but the ability to store mana into the blade itself and amplify its destructive output was above and beyond worth the risk—anything *to destroy things better.*

A perfect twin matched the blade at the other end of the handle. As someone who only cared about destroying things better and had eons to master their craft, I hardly gave a damn about the risks anymore.

I have no idea who they are or what they are talking about, but all shall be accompanied by death in the end. This world doesn't deserve to exist. The people don't need to suffer in it any longer.

Swiftly and mercilessly, I spun the blade between my fingers like a whirlwind before slicing the heads off the two daemons bowing before me.

"No doubt you're the monster... you would even cut down your own allies?!" I was greeted by another... visitor, their voice dripping with self-righteous indignation.

It seems a paladin has entered my demesne... full plate armor and a holy sword, blessed by a goddess, no doubt. And with him... an archer, a roguish fellow and... a heroine. Should I even be surprised? She is... quite gorgeous. Yet... she seems so familiar? It can't... Didn't she die? When? Was it before I became...

the Demon Lord? Why do I know that?! My head... it hurts. It's getting worse. I... can't...

I grasped my forehead tightly with my gauntlet, cutting into my flesh. Something... something was changing. *I* was changing, after so long...

The heroine shouted to her party; her voice echoed like a distant whisper in my ears.

"Something's wrong... he's in pain. We have to do something!"

I felt the presence of some gods and goddesses...

I hit the jackpot. With this much firepower, they could end it. But something was wrong. I couldn't focus anymore. What little clarity I had felt like it was slipping from me too...

Then, in a voice whose low rumble caused the ground and walls to shake, the monster spoke with the full force of its voice for the first time in millennia, almost possessed by a will that was not its own.

"My name is Sendrien Dagon, Demon Lord of Destruction. I am sorry, but this will be the end. Prepare yourselves. It is coming."

DOOM

Agh... Everything is going black.

Behind me, the magic array activated, unleashing the torrent of stored miasma. Millennia of it erupted with the fury of a raging flood as countless portals opened, connecting across the doomed world.

I could feel my body moving as if it was fighting independently, but I couldn't see anything. All I heard were the screams. This damned connection to the God of Darkness was throbbing unbearably. I couldn't resist it any longer.

...

...

"GRAND *PURIFICATION!*"

FUCK!

Searing pain ripped throughout my body as if a burning meteor had slammed me.

Sight returned to my eyes, with only the heroine left and almost everyone with her... dead. Brutally. In pieces. Everywhere. Except for one man, on the verge of death, hysterically crying, "He ate them! He ate all the gods! The darkness took them all! It's all over!"

Despite the wreckage left behind, I felt like a complete wreck. I doubted I could ever forget if I had felt like this before. My arm blades and their bones were broken just inches from my flesh. And my armor... was utterly shattered. *Damn.*

I liked that armor!

And... I couldn't see them.

Were my horns broken too? Yup.

My connection to the God of Darkness has been severely weakened. How? That spell... Grand Purification... it's...

I struggled with my memory while barely dodging another series of blows; sweat and blood dripped and splatted with each movement.

It's supposed to be a spell only able to be used by Legendary Heroes. The kind who can only be called by a high-ranking goddess facing a calamity. It's so hard to summon one; not even the war against the dragons qualified. Just what... am I now?

Desperation pervaded the heroine's eyes, carrying only a hint of hope. She was in as bad a state as the Demon Lord she fought.

"It worked! Hold on a little longer, Geralt, please! We can stop the Demon Lord transformation from completing!"

"Hahaha, even if... we stop it... all that miasma... will bring an unstoppable wave of demons... this is the end for us! Hahahaha!" The archer cackled madly, as blood poured out from his shoulder. The arm that should have been there was nowhere to be seen.

The... what? Demon Lord Transformation? Is that... me she is talking about? And the miasma will bring demons?!

I grimaced at the thought; it was something I would have to make better sense of when I actually had time to think about it.

A magic formation appeared beneath the heroine's feet; its sudden appearance caused her eyes to widen in shock. Any decent magic practitioner could tell what it was instantly: a summoning formation.

KILL! KILL! KILL HER NOW!

The voice in my head reverberated with incredible force, threatening my mind once again. I charged, catching her in the circle as it began to activate...

She didn't waste a moment, deciding against trying to escape from the formation, and instead, she clad her body in a white, holy aura. She screamed out once more, "*GRAND PURIFICATION!*" Simultaneously, I stabbed with my blade, enveloped in a thick, malevolent aura. Then, the world around us disappeared.

Chapter 1: My First Contract

THE YEAR OF EMPEROR HIRIHITO IV: 239

EMPIRE OF RIVELLION: CAPITAL CITY OF DYRRACHION

CONTINENT OF ANASTASIA

WORLD: GENOISIA

Dyrrachion, the Divine City, capital of the most populous empire in Genoisia. An expansive city, with developed land stretching almost as far as the eye could see. Even in such a metropolis, two structures stood out far more than any of the others.

One was the Imperial Palace, the pride of Rivellion, a project that took nearly one-hundred years to complete and cleared a mountain's worth of stone, steel, iron, and gold. It stood tall, shaped like a sword, with its highest spires cutting through the clouds in the sky.

The other was the Holy Temple, a sprawling complex built onto an expansive floating island that rivaled the height of the Imperial Palace, with opulent amounts of gold inlays designed to reflect its glory to all who could lay their eyes upon it. Eight thousand stairs floated in spirals from the ground through to the skies in order to reach the entrance, with shrines to each of the lesser deities interspersed on small floating islands along the route to the main island. Naturally, none of them could be considered comparable to the temples to the Great Deities residing on the main island.

In a hidden chamber deep within the Imperial Palace, numerous mages stood symmetrically around a summoning circle. A dozen large mana crystals were placed on eight points around the outer circle and on four points around the inner circle, with intricate mystical lines etched across the floor, connecting all the crystalline pillars.

"Balgruf, Is the summoning spell ready yet?"

"Yes, my Emperor. Everything is ready."

"Are you sure we can call a more competent hero with this? The idiot Ishtar sent us… He's a decent man, but we cannot leave our fate with him. You're aware of how troublesome it would be to lose the grace of the church if this fails?"

"Don't worry, my Emperor. We have checked over everything. We even used a powerful ritual to confirm the hero to summon beforehand. She can definitely save us. She was able to unite all the races in her world and defeated their world's Demon Lord. There should be no issues for them if we were to summon her, your grace."

"Very well. Then in the name of Hirihito IV, Emperor of Rivellion, I command you to execute the hero summoning at once!"

"Yes, my lord!" the mages responded in unison.

At the stroke of midnight, the mages began chanting their spell, and the circle flared with a fierce blue aura. The light shot into the sky and opened a portal perfectly aligned with the full moon.

However... as soon as the portal opened, an aura of despair descended upon the city. Its gravity was far greater than anything they could have imagined. The sky itself cracked and shattered, as the blue aura of the portal burst outward, inundated with scarlet and crimson colors.

"Balgruf, what is going on?! You said this was planned perfectly!"

"I don't know! The spell was set to call the heroine, it shouldn't have targeted anything else! Quick, stop the summoning!"

Some of the mages desperately tried to end the ritual as fear clouded their eyes and the weight of the tear across the sky pressed down upon them. Others stared at the portal in the sky, rooted in place by sheer terror. Only Balgruf and the emperor manage to maintain their calm.

"Depth of spirit, our hearts call upon you, follow our commands, let the mana find peace and rest. *Antimagic Field*!"

A sphere emanated around the portal, as grey energy futilely tried to inject itself into the array. It barely managed to lessen the weight of the aura enveloping them. Despite their attempts to sever the flow of magic, the ritual circle alighted with crackles of lightning as the mana concentrations grew ever fiercer within the portal far above.

Then... a bright white light erupted at the portal with a thunderous impact. The horrendous weight and imposing aura collapsed to a fraction of its former impact, and rapidly decreased as it's source was flung at incredible speeds across the night sky and was lost in the distance. However, crashing into the middle of the circle was their heroine, bloodied and impaled through the heart by a sinister black blade.

As suddenly as it had begun, the world fell to calm again, and the portal slowly began to fade away.

Choking on blood, she barely coughed out her dying words, "I... did it... I sa... ve... him..."

Emperor Hirihito stared at the heroine's lifeless body as if marveling for a moment, then snapped back to reality as his eyes shot blades into Balgruf.

While Balgruf was covered in a cold sweat, hands trembling violently, he was still able to keep himself composed enough, at least when compared to the cries of terror from his fellow mages. He knew things had gone truly bad when even Emperor Hirihito, renowned for his extreme composure, displayed a slight shaking in his hands, perhaps for the first time in his life.

It only showed itself for a moment, before Hirihito regained his composure. Although he couldn't cover up a slight quiver in his voice, he did not hesitate to shout out commands to regain a semblance of control over the situation.

"This blade... I can already feel its power... as if it is reaching into my very soul. Balgruf, check to see if it is cursed and investigate what powers it has! If it is safe to use, we may yet have a weapon which can turn the tide of the war, and potentially mitigate this disaster. Do not fail me a second time. I need to speak with the captain of the Knight's Order to investigate what happened with that ominous aura. MESSENGER! Come here now, we must send for the Saintess immediately. This... will be difficult, but this issue needs to be smoothed over with the church before it gets too far out of hand!"

With a swish of his cape, the emperor turned and left the room, his internal turmoil only growing worse.

I only meant to help our people! How... how did it turn out like this?!

Balgruf stared for a moment, the dark aura from the blade felt almost as if it called to him, and the magecite that was blended into it started shining in various colors. It was... enthralling. He was so focused on the blade itself that he did not notice that the aura flowing from the blade glided off the skin of the fallen heroine, who looked almost like an angel bound in darkness. Balgruf started shouting orders to the surrounding mages, before unceremoniously pulling the blade from her body.

Almost as an afterthought, he waved for an attendant to remove the heroine's body and to send it for burial, as he hastily returned to his study while his eyes glowed with unfettered greed. As a simple matter of course, he also grabbed a map of Anastasia. The Knight's Order was certain to ask him where that... *thing* had gone, and he had no mind to allow anything to distract him from studying his new toy. *Blast... what if it flew all the way to Luthas?*

Balgruf shuddered a moment. *It'd be fine. The king of Luthas and the Emperor are on favorable terms, as long as we handle this problem quickly and smoothly...*

Across the city, streets that were usually empty by this hour filled with people, eyes turned upward and praying to their gods to deliver them from this ill omen. Others stayed at home, cowering in the deepest corners they could find, hiding from the scarlet light emanating from the now red moon.

Kingdom of Luthas, Eastern Anastasia
Borders: Sea of Calimnon to the east and the Archipelago of the Feylands

Duke Vermillion carefully turned the pages of a report; a small, lonely pile of white settled perfectly centered across a rigid sea of black marble that made up the Duke's working desk. When he wasn't holding court or hosting an official meeting, this was ostensibly the best place to find him.

Occasionally, he would look over the edge and glare down at the messenger, kneeling with his head lowered and trembling slightly. The Duke smirked, as the few extra stairs between his office and the reception area made the man below look truly small. He was especially fond of emphasizing the difference in status, a point he emphasized here to a lesser degree than his throne room. He eyed the man's head with ferocious intent, only for the man to shiver and lower it further.

Good. This cretin knows his place.

Duke Vermillion furrowed his brow, the slight rustling of paper disturbing the otherwise interminable silence as he raised the report for closer inspection.

"Messenger, come. Bring me the fifth book on the third shelf from the right, in the middle row." The Duke casually broke the silence, and waved nonchalantly towards the shelves to his left without as much as a glance.

"Yes, my lord!" The messenger leapt up, grateful for the reprieve as he hustled up the stairs. He gazed for a moment at the numerous shelves that lined the walls, and blanched slightly. The middle shelf... while perhaps within reach for someone of the Duke's stature, was surely much too high for him to reach. His eyes darted around frantically, and then relaxed slightly as he spied a three-tier step ladder folded in the corner.

"One, two, three..." The messenger muttered under his breath, pointing as he counted across the shelves before aligning and climbing the ladder.

"Uh... a-apologies, my lord, but which fifth book did you wa-"

"I said the fifth, don't make me repeat myself." The Duke didn't even proffer a glance in the messenger's direction, albeit he did smirk ever so slightly.

There were ten books lining this shelf... and, at a glance, all the shelves seemed to have an even number of book. After squirming for a moment, the messenger grabbed and brought both fifth books. One was titled *An Ecological Report of the Western Mountains*, and the other, older book *James Hawthorne's Examination of the Tribal Nation's in the Northern Wilds*.

The messenger quickly hurried back around to the front of the Duke's desk, and bowed with both books in his outstretched arms. He shuddered slightly as the Duke glared for half a moment, clicked his tongue, and then took both books from his hands.

"Good. Now go fetch *my* council, and send them to meet me here. You are dismissed." With a snap of his fingers, a scroll bearing the duke's seal danced its way out of one of the drawers and floated neatly into the messenger's freshly freed hand.

"Yes, my lord!" The messenger raised his head, thumped his fist against his chest in a salute, and hurried out of the study as fast as he could manage without making any appearance of disrespect.

As he waited, Vermillion quickly skimmed through both books. Each time he stopped, he would nod to himself before swishing his fingers across the page as a small, thin blue cloth manifested itself and nestled perfectly in the crook of the book.

"Perhaps…" the duke murmured to himself, as a cold smirk etched its way across his face, "I can finally rid myself of that resilient little stain after all… The Count's timing couldn't have been any better!"

Somewhere near the northern village of Kurstwood:

A half dozen knights lead a small carriage down the road, drawn by two weary horses. A young, ten year-old girl rode inside with an older mage, who looked to be in his late sixties, with a long white beard. She also kept with her a bodyguard, who wore leather armor and sported a scruffy brown beard. He was much younger than the mage, in his early thirties at the oldest. He was also the leader of her knights. The glint off the hilt of her small rapier accented the otherwise dark demeanor of her deep purple dress.

Her family crest was clearly visible on the right side of her chest, with a red and gold shield broken into four quadrants. Two of the quadrants had symbols of golden wyverns, while the other two had symbols of a lyre harp and a knight.

"Gregory, how much longer until we reach Kurstwood?" the girl asked.

"We are just a day out now, have patience Lady Diane," the knight responded.

Her impatience earned a scoff from the old mage. "Hmph. No need to still play along, Gregory. We both know why her father is sending our young lady on such a dangerous and understaffed investigation."

Gregory chided back, "Hal, that's the point. She's only ten. At least try to let her feel a little peace!"

Diane quickly protested, "Hey, I'm still right here, you know! And… I already know. I already know. I don't need things to be sugarcoated for me."

Diane leaned back in her seat, her eyes drawn back to the window, their azure color carried a surprising weight for someone so young.

Gregory and Hal glanced at each other, and collectively sighed. They felt a little ashamed at bringing the issue up again. Succession disputes in noble houses are never a pretty thing, and they had been placed on the losing end. Ever since Lady Diane was diagnosed as incompatible with magic, her father and both of her older brothers and sisters wanted her out of the family. Her eldest sister's otherwise general indifference to her existence was the closest thing to kindness, compared to the rest of her family's open hostility.

In this country, those with the most ability gained the inheritance rights. However, the family was still required to support the non-inheriting members. Furthermore, back in a brighter period of the kingdom, killing family members was outlawed and numerous protections were given to protect the lives of nobles from their cutthroat politics. Amongst noble families, prestige meant everything. If a family were to refuse to support one of their children, the other families would use that as an opportunity to discredit their rivals and move up the social ladder.

However, having a child that was incompatible with magic created the exact same problem, as they were considered a stain on the family's honor. Even though removing them from the inheritance was a relatively easy maneuver, they would continue to sap the family funds and bring shame upon the them. Thus, great noble families would strain to find any circumstance they could to remove such problems while maintaining the façade of supporting such incompetents.

Despite her being brought up in such an environment, Hal couldn't help but smile a moment as he recalled when he was first rescued by Lady Diane. Compared to the other magic-less children of noble families, she had a fair amount of luck and a tenacious spirit that carried her through her family's plots to rid themselves of her.

A little over two years ago, Diane's father had found Hal's aging and weakening magic to be unbefitting of a man in his station. Conjuring up the first excuse he could find, Duke Vermillion had Hal beaten and cast into the streets, timing it with an unseasonably cold and strong storm no less. Injured, alone, and in the rain and hail, no matter how strong he used to be, *he should have died.*

But... he wanted to live! He'd spent his entire life trying to escape the limits of his birth, and only after a brief moment in the sun, he had been cast aside as a useless rag!

It was then that Diane found him... she was only four years old at the time, and kept only a single servant, an old maid far past her years and at the end of her life. To think, that by that point in her life, she had already been forced to escape from a couple of bandit encounters. She barely made it out alive through luck or by the grace of good-hearted passersby. All the other servants she had been assigned before had abandoned or betrayed her.

Yet she was the only one to come to Hal while he was at his worst, bleeding in the pouring rain. She reached out her little hand and welcomed him and his aged bones into her carriage, still able to cry at the plight of another. Amid the tears and her rudimentary speech, she demanded that he serve her loyally and be a good man. That was it. The loneliness and fear and weakness of her life made Diane into the one halfway decent noble Hal had ever met, and he has met many in his time in the duke's service.

It wasn't long after that when Diane picked up Sir Gregory, then Tront, Garen, Frank and Sam. She found each of them at the lowest point in their lives, abandoned, driven out, injured, *alone*. Each time she refined her speech bit by bit, as she learned bigger and better words. As her motley crew grew larger and stronger, her father began to send her on more and more dangerous missions. Even if his abilities had greatly waned from his peak, Hal was more than glad to use his years of experience to spite the duke. Despite her attitude, as far as Hal was concerned, this little girl had a heart of gold and was the best thing to come out of that family. She was almost like the daughter he had dreamed of having.

However, this mission was, by far, the most vexing one yet.

Hal couldn't help but scrunch his face in consternation.

Kurstwood. A small village at the edge of a dangerous wilderness, with travelers few and far between. Only traders with a few adventurers leave there once every week to come and sell their goods and assorted monster parts in the ducal capital. Those adventurers reported that something had started to rile up the local monsters, and soon after, Kurstwood missed their delivery. This kind of investigation requires much more than just us, even if it is our assigned territory.

clack clack

clack clack

thunk

The wheel, as it jarred and bounced over a somewhat larger-than-average rock, stirred Diane from her silent staring contest with the forest, and she noticed something... or rather, someone in the bushes.

She perked up with a shout, "Hey, there is someone hurt in those thistle bushes over there!"

"What?!" Gregory exclaimed. In an abundance of caution, he commanded their entourage, despite the fact one could clearly see they already knew the drill. "Knights, quickly, alert positions!"

clack clack

clack clack

clank clank

clank clank

The distant sound of hooves and armor caused Dagon to stir in the prickly bush that had been his resting place for the past week. Compared to the intimidating form he held before, his body had shrunk in size and was coated from head to toe in dried blood and grime, not to mention the numerous deep wounds from his battle with the heroine.

Finally some people! I think... I can hear a girl yelling... damn! How can I pull off a contract with this many people around? If I can't bind my spirit here, I really will die... that spell is really nasty... it has been this long and I still haven't regained my healing... Just a little more mana... to adjust my eyes to look more human...

"Alright men, ready up, the little lady is at it again!" Gregory called. "Someone clear the back of the carriage!"

"Haha, let's see what speech she has prepared this time!" Tront replied.

"Hey, this is no time for jokes, keep your eyes on the perimeter," Hal said. "I'll be damned if we get caught by bandits again."

I can hear them debating... what are they going on about? A speech? Bandits? Ah... that makes some sense.

As the carriage pulled close to the roadside, Diane flung open the door and stood with all the pride and authority a child could attempt to bear. She tried hard to distract from the irrefutable fact that she was small enough to easily stand in the doorway of her carriage.

"I am Lady Diane of House Culaine, heir to the village of Kurstwood! If you swear absolute loyalty to me and always listen to me and promise to be my best friend forever and to never hurt me or anyone ever, I promise you we will help you!" She puffed out her chest as she spoke, trying to emulate as much grandeur as she could muster.

Dagon's eyes widened in surprise as his thoughts raced through his mind.

What the hell is this? Is this my penance? What kind of speech is this? This sounds like it can be used as the terms of a contract, but a contract is absolute. I can't argue these terms if I want to live. The first time I will ever fall under a contract... and it is with this oddly familiar little brat... still, I have lived through far worse. And humans are incredibly fragile, short-lived creatures. Compared to how long I have had to tolerate that shitty god's voice...

And... strange. I haven't heard that voice since I arrived here. I don't feel it... Was the connection broken?

Damnit! I don't have the time to worry about that, especially since this is the risky part. In order to execute a binding contract, I have to use my true name. The guards will likely kill me at that point. Not that it matters. Here we go.

With a cough, he cleared some of the excess blood from his lungs, adding another small splotch to the tapestry adorned his now pathetic state.

"Heh. Well then, Lady Diane, I, Sendrien Dagon, the last king of house Dagon, and... Demon Lord of Destruction, accept your terms and bind my soul to your oath."

Sendrien's eyes twitched as he referred to himself as a Demon Lord... it was something that voice had used to refer to itself, not one he chose for himself. However, for the oath, it was better to be sure than to risk it.

Sam immediately keeled over in laughter. "Hahahaha! Not even peasants on the verge of death take her seriously or believe who she is! Let's just move ahead to Kurstwood, that guy's not long for this world anyways."

A smile broke out on Gregory's face.

"Pffft. Hahaha! Sam, did you forget? The reason all of us follow this audacious girl is that she picked up strays like us when we were at our worst. And last I remember, she gave you this exact same speech when we saved you from those back-alley thugs! You couldn't have looked much better than this kid, and I don't recall you laughing then. Did you forget your wailing, snotty thanks?"

"Hahhhh? W-well, that was then! And I didn't make fun of her! Damn, look! I, we need to keep up our security posture!"

The knights laughed while Sam, completely red-faced, stormed off to the roadside and feigned watching for activity across the sparsely forested field.

Strange. Is it because I am so weak right now? The contract feels like it was executed, but I see no signs of the seal. Seems I got lucky. Thankfully they can't tell I am a demon. I get to live. Where even is this? It looks nothing like what I remember of my world... I know I left nothing safe. Does that mean... my whole plan was in vain? I killed off everything... and yet life goes on. Pain and suffering will continue. Have I... failed?

"Shut it, you guys! This is important! And you, enough of the demon play! Since you don't want to tell me your name, your name is now Thistleman, since I found you in a thistle bush and you're a guy! Gregory, pick him up. We are gonna treat him and take him with us." Diane chided the knight's sharply, which only provoked more laughter out of them.

What the hell is with this broken logic?! How... how do I have no other choices?!

"I see... Thistle... man... Huh," Dagon quietly muttered, barely holding on against his exhaustion.

Hal raised his eyebrows and watched Dagon like a hawk, an odd expression etching its way across his face. After looking back at Diane, and the determination and pity that emanated from her face, he decided to not voice his concerns aloud.

Does this mean they think I am a peasant from Kurstwood? That... that's the town that was burning when I first crashed here, right? Why the hell are they going there?!

As Gregory stepped away to grab a cleaning rag, Dagon closed his eyes. He surrendered to his fate, too weak, too bloodied, and too tired to keep fighting it. Other small adjustments began to take hold of his body, imperceptible beneath the layers of blood and grime. His skin color turned to match that of Diane's, and his eyes did not revert to their demon form. Even the signs of age on his skin regressed.

A small hand wiped the blood and grime from his face, revealing the large gashes underneath along with the visage of a youthful boy.

To find such a thing caused the surrounding knights to react with shock. Only Hal seemed unsurprised at the turn of events.

"Hey! Shit, he's just a boy!" Tront said. "How the hell did a kid survive with wounds like these? My god... what the hell happened to him?"

"Hal, hurry with the recovery magic, will you!" Gregory called. "The young lady is crying for him, so at least give it a try! Damn old fogey!"

"You don't think... all that blood was actually his own?!? That's insane!" Garen said.

"I'm coming, I'm coming," Hal huffed. "Gah! I can't rush like the old days anymore..."

As Hal started preparing his spell, a small chuckle escaped his lips.

"Ahhh... I just remembered a good word to describe our Lady Diane, I can't really recall the foreigner who taught it to me... but I believe she is quite the Tsundere, eh? Haha!"

Hal cocked an eye towards the unconscious Thistleman, and whispered under his breath, "You're the weirdest one yet... and now you're in for one helluva ride. Guess we are too."

Chapter 2:
Kurstwood

Dusk has settled in as they approached the edge of Kurstwood. Groves of evergreen pines thickened along both sides of the road, accentuating the gloom. The area had an unnatural silence about it. No more birds could be seen in the dying light, not even a silhouette. More notable was the pervasive silence that replaced the usual hum of cicadas and the northern treehoppers. Nor was there any sign that anybody had traveled on this road in over a week.

The cool, clammy weather and poor, rocky soil bordering the Hawthorne wilderness were not conducive to growing anything but small patches of the hardiest crops, and even then, their yields were often very poor. Located on the edge of a wilderness filled with hostile demi-human tribes, only the hardiest people or those seeking to hide out from the kingdom's enforcers would try and make a living here.

They rounded a turn in the road and the low wooden walls of Kurstwood came into view, spurring audible gasps from the knights outside the carriage.

One of the knights rushed to the side of the carriage.

"Sir Gregory, it is much worse than we feared! The town... it has been completely destroyed..."

"What?!" Gregory exclaimed, before leaping out of the carriage. "Hal, watch after the lady and the boy. Tront, Garen—you two stay with them. We are too exposed out here, so head to the village center, there should be a garrison outpost there. That is where we will set up camp. The rest of you, with me! We need to look for more survivors to find out what happened here."

"Sir, shouldn't we send someone back to report on this?" Tront's voice failed to conceal a quiver of fear as he eyed the damage.

"Going back to that bastard of a duke on your own would be no different than if none of us made it back at all. Only difference being you would find yourself in a lonely spot on a gallows or in the bottom of a lake. He already knew something was wrong, why do you think he sent us first?" Hal's voice hardened, as his wizened old eyes scanned all around them.

"Enough chatter, let get moving!" Gregory commanded with a hint of exasperation.

"Sir, yes sir!" The knights responded in unison.

As Gregory, Frank and Sam hurried ahead, Hal stepped out from the carriage as well.

"Lady Diane, stay inside the carriage until I tell you it is safe to come out. I will be riding up front with the coachman. If you need anything, just open the front panel and let me know."

Hal's serious tone and hardened look conveyed the importance of his command. Diane quietly nodded as she looked anxiously into the ruined village ahead. After Hal exited the carriage, she thought she saw an ominous dark aura in the village before it suddenly disappeared. She shook her head vigorously and looked again, seeing only the same wreckage.

Maybe it was just her mind playing tricks on her because of her anxiety? She couldn't see auras. Only people who had a mana heart could see auras, and she was one of those rare people who was born crippled. *Incompetent*, they liked to say. She had never seen nor felt magic, as much as she wished to and as hard as she tried.

Diane's failures pranced through her memories like a mosquito that just wouldn't stop buzzing in her ears, the laughter of her older siblings, and the look of disdain in her father's eyes. She clutched her little fists tighter. *Is your stupid status and my marginal inheritance so important that I don't get the right to live too? And even that's been taken from me...*

Ahead of the group, the gate had clearly been smashed through. Long sections of the wall were burnt and shattered, splintered and charred logs and posts were scattered far from their respective sections.

The inside of the village was not any better. Houses lay in ruins, some still slightly smoldering. As they proceeded closer to the village center, it became more and more clear that an atrocity had happened here. In spite of not finding a single body, blood stained large swathes of the road and the walls of the surrounding buildings. There were more broken barricades and a lot more blood. A large hole had been pierced through the walls of the garrison outpost.

Hal muttered, "This is absolutely no good. This whole place reeks of death... and whatever came through, it finished everyone off here."

Tront and Garen shivered, drawing their quaking swords as they scanned wide-eyed all around.

"Hal, this is obviously very bad! Whatever happened... This should be enough, right? We really should leave now, please? Please?!" Tront begged.

"Tront, we can't leave yet," Hal replied. "If we don't find out what invaded and killed these people, we won't be able to make adequate preparations. Even the duke has to take this seriously. At the very least, we have to wait for Sir Gregory to make it back before we can leave. Keep the carriage at the ready in the center, and let's start fixing up some of these barricades." Hal quickly barked out orders, before getting to work himself. Tront and Garen looked at each other apprehensively, before nodding and getting to work.

Gregory and his knights maneuvered carefully through the rubble of the village near the wall.

"Helloooo! Is anyone still here? We are knights of House Culaine. We are here to help!" Gregory called; his voice met with nothing but an eerie silence.

After half an hour of searching, the dark of night fell upon the village. Gregory stopped shouting. The more they searched, the deeper their fear gnawed inside them. Only the light of their torches kept their terror at bay. Their senses were fully primed, on edge, and any chatter fell to silence as they strained their ears on every creak or brush of the wind.

After another hour of cautious searching, they had nearly finished circling most of the village. Frank hurriedly approached Gregory, while still attempting to keep a low profile.

"Sir... I think I heard something in the inn across the street there," the knight whispered, his eyes stretched wide and darted constantly around him.

"Alright, let's check it out." Gregory nodded, then waved his torch to catch Sam's attention. "Everyone, on me. Swords drawn. Frank, watch our backs."

As he approached the inn, Gregory smelled it before he heard it, the sharp scent of fresh blood.

CRUNCH!

Gregory shuddered, and he swallowed hard before mustering the courage to look in the window. His face immediately paled.

"L-l-l-l-lesser demon... grendel... The hell is a demon doing here?!" he whispered.

A tall, gangly demon was hunched over in the inn. It had long arms with sharp claws and brown, leathery skin. Its head had two small horns protruding from the top and its eyes had two slotted pupils, similar to those of a goat. The arm of woman protruded from its mouth, blood seeping out between its teeth as it chewed.

Gregory motioned for the knights to back off. The demon glanced at the inn walls with one of its large eyes, where the torchlight danced for a moment before disappearing.

Gregory hurried down the road towards the village center with his knights in tow.

"Hurry, we need to meet up with Lady Diane and Hal and get out of here! We would need at least a hundred soldiers to defeat a grendel!" Gregory shouted between breaths.

"This is bad sir, really bad! Grendels are part of the Demon Lord's forces, aren't they? They shouldn't be here! They should still be in Ebenheim, on the other side of the sea!" Frank shouted back, pale with fear.

"I don't know why it is here, just the fact that it is here is bad enough! We need—"

Gregory was cut off mid-sentence as Sam screeched in agony. He swiftly looked back and saw the long claws stabbed straight through the heart of the knight. The grendel opened its hand slowly, almost in amusement, splitting Sam effortlessly in half.

Gregory yelled, "Frank, run and get Lady Diane out of here! I'll hold it here to buy them some time!"

Gregory readied his sword, sweat coating his palms, before he charged towards the demon.

Frank dropped his sword and torch as he sprinted towards the village center as fast as he could manage. Behind him, he heard more loud crunches and screaming, followed by a monstrous shriek. Adrenaline and fear spurred him on even faster. He could see the barricades up ahead, lit by a small ring of torches. Hal and the others were looking towards him, their faces paled.

Frank tried to scream "Run" but he couldn't... and then he no longer felt the ground under his feet. He was suddenly high up in the air. Blood gurgled out of his mouth. He looked down, greeted by a large claw shoved unceremoniously through his chest. His pendant was pierced open, as his blood dripped onto the photo of his wife and son and tears began to rain from his contorted face.

The horses neighed uncontrollably, rearing up and snapping at their harnesses. The coachman was desperately trying to calm them, while replacing the damaged pieces.

"Damnit, something is spooking the horses! At this rate, we won't be able to move the carriage out of here!"

Lady Diane looked out the window at Hal, who sat next to Garen and a small fire. Tront patrolled around the barriers.

"Hal, when do you think Gregory is going to make it back here? I'm getting worried," Diane called out to her old mentor.

"Hah, he is an experienced knight. He knows what he is doing. He will be back soon. How's your new friend doing?"

"It seems like he is recovering, some more color is coming back to his skin. You said he will be fine, right?"

Hal had a pensive look on his face. Without a doubt, even with his treatment, that boy should have died. No human should have been able to survive those wounds. Even then, something more was off about it, he just hadn't had the heart yet to tell the young lady. While he could not believe the boy was a Demon Lord, as there had never been more than one Demon Lord alive at any one time, something about what he said was strange. The more he thought about it, the more concerning it was. You could take it as a joke… but for a dying kid to actually joke like that? However, that wasn't a problem for now. He would deal with it later.

Hal shook himself from his thoughts. "Hmm? Oh, Yes, yes indeed. He will certainly be well enough. Although I doubt a peasant like him will stick around once he comes to. Peasants are notorious for not keeping their word, as they live worlds apart from nobles like you."

"Hal, that's just so mean! Why would they do that? That shouldn't matter, and he promised to be my friend… I will hold him to his promise!"

Hal shifted uncomfortably. He would have to be careful as he felt it would be safer to get rid of the boy. Whatever the kid's case was, it would likely only bring more trouble. The more he thought about it, the more he didn't like it.

Then they all heard a blood curdling scream.

"Tront, Garen, at the ready! Man the barricade. Coachman, get those damn horses ready! Diane, stay inside!"

Hal prepared his staff in one hand and a talisman in the other. He started chanting and the talisman burned with an orange flame, shooting out a small force field to reinforce the barriers on the eastern road. *I may be old, but I'll be damned if I let anything take me down easily!*

Hal braced himself, his mouth turned to a cold grimace.

They heard a second scream, and then a horrendous shriek.

"Coachman, are the horses not ready yet?!"

"I am trying! I got one reharnessed, but they are going wild! It's too much on my own!"

Before he could respond, Hal saw Frank emerge from the shadows in absolute panic, and behind him a large, tall outline. A claw pierced through Frank's chest, and raised him up nearly ten feet in the air, blood pouring out of his chest and mouth. A large maw laced with sharp, vicious teeth emerged from the darkness.

CRUNCH!

His head was gone. The demon flung the body back on to the ground, shattering lifeless limbs while eyeing the remaining knights.

Fucking Tront jinxed it! Hal glared furiously, as he scrambled to think of a way to turn things around.

"I DON'T GIVE A DAMN HOW YOU DO IT, BUT GET THEM UNDER CONTROL NOW!" Hal screamed at the coachmen, his voice cracking with the force of his shout.

Things had just gotten really, really bad.

Chapter 3: Awakening

"Garen, Tront! Buy me time! Strike its arms when it attacks the barrier!"

Hal barked his commands as quickly as he could, then immediately started chanting an incantation. Lightning sprung into existence and swirled on the tip of his staff.

The grendel slowly emerged from the darkness. Gregory's longsword protruded from its eye as a sickly yellow vitreous gel dripped out; the fiend glared for but a moment before it unleashed a terrible bellow.

"Fuckin' hells! It got the captain too!" Garen yelled as he rushed into position.

The demon rushed forward and swung at Tront, its claw clashing against the barrier, unable to pierce through it. The knights swung in kind at the grendel's outstretched arm, and Garen's blade landed a deep cut. He grunted with exertion, but he couldn't yank it back out. The grendel howled again and ripped back its arm before biting the blade in half.

The creature unleashed a visceral howl, swiping relentlessly at the barrier, bashing it again and again. The barrier managed to hold, each blow repulsed just like the last. Tront stumbled back, trembling in fear. He screamed, "We're gonna die. It's going to kill us. Oh god, help us!"

"Hold firm, fool! My spell is almost ready!" Hal attempted to reassure him as firmly and confidently as he could.

Hal's mind raced far faster than his body could keep up. *Damn my age! Damn my weakness! It takes so long for me to prepare a spell of just this level! If I had the mana, I could unleash this much faster! This is bad... If I don't land this just right... Just a little more...*

"Call forth from the formless sky, let loose thy blinding flash of light, from afar, let all shudder at your roar..." Hal chanted, focusing upon the rabid beast before him.

The grendel stopped swinging at the barrier and looked at Hal with a malicious level of intelligence, while lightning swirled ferociously around his staff. Then, it squatted low before launching itself over the barrier.

It landed directly in front of Hal, blood and saliva dripping from its mouth onto the mage's mortified face.

"*T-t-t-THUNDERBOLT!*" Hal stuttered as he cut his chant far too short.

There was no more time. He unleashed all the energy he had accumulated and it struck Gregory's sword, sending the electricity straight into the demon. It screamed in agony, wildly swinging at Hal. The old man was thrown like a ragdoll as the claws raked through and eviscerated him, spilling out his guts and splattering fresh viscera across the bloodied cobblestone.

"HAAAAL! NOOOOO!!!" Diane screeched at the top of her lungs, her hands digging tightly into the carriage's window as her eyes opened wide in horror. That old man had been the closest thing she had to a father.

Tront shrieked in terror; he spun around and stabbed with all his might, and managed to pierce the demon's leg with his sword. The grendel howled again, and turned towards its prey that fled with all its might. Diane hurled herself from the carriage, pointing her hands towards the demon.

She cried out again and again in fury and pain, tears welling in her eyes. "*Fireball! Fireball! Fireball!* Please... Work! Work! *FIREBALL!*"

Without their swords and the protection of the barrier, Tront and Garen were less than lambs brought to slaughter before the monster. They tried to yell out something to her, but she couldn't hear them. Her eyes were full of tears and her heart felt nothing but pain and rage.

❧ • ☙

The world was darkness. Sendrien tried to raise his hand in front of his face... and still saw nothing. He scrunched his eyes sharply as he held his head, and then relaxed in the silence.

Appreciating the silence for a moment longer, he allowed himself a long sigh. *When was the last time my mind felt so... quiet? What if the voice returned?* Perish the thought.

His mind wandered in the silence. With the most pressing matters dealt with, he soon became troubled by a flood of his own thoughts. *The hell did I get myself into to? That damn hero... I can't remember if I was ever left in a state worse than this after a fight. Hell, I'll live, so I suppose it was worth it... Still, why did she seem so familiar?*

He groaned at the thought, his hand tightening on his head with enough strength to draw a little more blood.

I wonder what this will be like? To do such a thing... A contract, huh. Me? I can't believe I've been reduced to the games those cowards loved to play...

Remember... I need to remember... what else did those fey bastards say about contracts? They can bind your souls, that I know for sure, but what else did they say? Contractors... should be able to sense each other, I think? Damn it, I should have paid more attention to those stupid details.

Dagon exhaled deeply and slowly, as invisible tendrils of mana danced outward from his body and flowed into the carriage. It twisted itself into something, but it was just so weak. Abysmal. *Pathetic.* There was hardly a trace of magic to it. Why?

The tendrils grew in strength as they probed deeper, and began to move away, and slowly took on a more concrete form of Diane's silhouette. The magic circuits etched throughout her body began to alight, albeit dimly. *Why are they empty?* The tendrils of mana pressed into her mana circuits, shriveled and weak as they were from disuse, snaking their way towards a tiny blackened speck near her heart that emanated only the smallest amounts of blue mana.

Is this... her mana heart? It looked almost like... someone or something had blocked it up. A disease? A genetic disorder? Or something else?

"Unacceptable." I muttered venomously. *My first contract, and my contractor can't even use magic?!*

Maybe if I filled her mana heart to overflowing, it would burst through the blockage. Or would that hurt her? I'd only recovered a little bit, but even a small amount of my mana could be overwhelming to her. She was still such a small child. Ten years, was it? Sendrien's grimace only deepened.

His hand darted down to clench his chest, as Dagon's eyes shot open and his teeth clenched, withholding another groan. *What the hell is this? This pain... no... this isn't coming from my chest. It's external. Is this a side-effect of the contract? Is this her pain? Why is she in pain?*

Tendrils of mana scattered far and wide in a silent, invisible burst. Closing his eyes, the outlines of the village illuminated themselves in shadowy form.

Ah... I see the problem. Risks be damned, there's no way I'll break my promise and let this shitty little pissant kill my first contractor. Let's get this little lady some mana, yeah?

An unnatural fiendish grin crossed Dagon's childish face, and the tendrils of mana began to swell, darken and flow with a hellish fervor. *It's as much as a pebble in a mountain range, but it'll have to do.*

The grendel finished killing the two remaining knights.

It didn't know why, it just knew that it had to fulfill his master's will. Plus, these humans were both soft and crunchy. They sated his hunger. There was one left, and the horses.

Between them and the other remaining bodies, it would be able to feast for a little while longer. Maybe it could even grow some?

It turned around and saw the little girl screaming at him. She would make a nice treat. Only one thing left to do.

badump badump

The grendel froze. It had never felt anything like that before.

It looked at the little girl, its body shaking. It felt... fear?

This girl... why does she have an aura of death?

The rapidly growing dark cloud shook the grendel to its core, and it made it feel so small! A towering daemonic aura, and within it a face straight from the depths of hell—growing, spreading, and *furiously* emanating from this little girl! Steam burst from her soft, reddening flesh in unison with the growing cloud. At her hands, a glow formed, spiraling, coalescing, gathering into an effervescent ball of liquid flame. The heat from the flames was enough to sear the grendel from a dozen feet away. It turned, it wanted to run, but it was far too late.

"*FIREBALL!*"

The last thing it heard was the roar, the earth shaking beneath its feet. It couldn't escape. The ball of flame crashed into its back, sending searing flame through its flesh and bone as it carried the grendel several hundred feet down the road before it exploded, incinerating everything in indiscriminate fury. A light as bright as the sun flashed outward, follow by a tremendous roar. Shattered pieces of the village were sent hurtling into the forest beyond, their flames setting the forest ablaze.

Diane felt as if something exploded inside of her. Her entire body felt as if it was burning, energy roiling through her. She could hardly concentrate. Fire burst from her hands. Then a quarter of the village… was gone in flames.

And just as suddenly as it came, the overwhelming energy was gone. She felt empty, unable to concentrate, overtaken by extreme exhaustion. Diane collapsed, her body broiling as her vision shuddered into a thick haze.

After the explosion quieted down, the coachman crawled out from under the carriage.

"W-w-what just happened? Is it gone?"

He looked around. The horses huddled together, frozen in fear. He decided it wasn't worth the time to investigate the village, and instead took the opportunity to re-harness the other horse. One last quick glance, and he saw Lady Diane collapsed on the ground. Her body was the only one not doused in its own blood, the last traces of steam fading away.

"Ah! My lady! Are yah hurt?"

He sprinted up to her and heard her labored breathing. With a grunt, he lifted the young child and placed her back inside the carriage. The dancing lights of the flames accentuated the deep red hue that consumed all her skin that could be seen.

I may be old, but I'll be damned if I just abandoned the young lady like this! Never underestimate a coachman's honor!

He puffed out his chest with a bit of pride. If nothing else, he would always see his clients to their destination, no matter what! Otherwise... well, he'd be out of a job. And he frankly had no idea how to do much else well enough to live off it. Nor could he take the blame for abandoning a noble. Even if that was what her father wanted... he and his family would still be executed just for that bastard to keep up appearances.

"Hiya! Move ye horses!"

The creatures whinnied and began an eager gallop out of the village; they were all too happy to put the place behind them as fast as they could.

The carriage jostled rapidly back through the broken gates and onto the worn road.

And tah make sure I keep my coachman's honor for a long time yet, I am NEVER doin' one-ah these dangerous jobs again!

Chapter 4: Versailles

Clack clack clack... thunk! Clack clack clack clack.

The carriage wheel bounced off a large stone near the side of the road. The jolting jarred Thistleman awake, his head rebounding like a rubber ball bouncing off the hard wood of the carriage.

"Ah! Ow ow ow, ahh that smarts!" Thistle cradled his head in between his arms, with everything feeling a lot more sensitive than usual.

He glanced over at Diane, sprawled on the seat. Her breathing was quite uneven, although not quite pained. Thistleman snaked out his aura to study her body, breathing a sigh of relief to find no damage. She was getting fairly dehydrated though.

Reveal Mana.

He watched a chaotic flurry of mana particles course through Diane's mana heart. Pulsating. Swirling. Colliding. Yet still slowly moving towards balance. A consequence of her sudden awakening? It seemed to be consuming her entire mind to adjust and acclimate to her new reality.

She needed water though. And if her labored breathing was any indicator of how much focus the acclimation and mana regulation was taking, then just pouring some water down the poor kid's throat would be intensely problematic. The mind needed to adapt to the overwhelming amount of new information.

Although, if I just used some mana to guide some water down her throat... then it shouldn't be an issue.

Satisfied with his solution, he then moved on to other matters.

Thistleman opened the curtain. The resplendent reds and oranges of the setting sun slowly faded towards dusk. The low hum of insects weaved a peaceful song for the evening. He noticed that the carriage was slowly drifting towards the edge of the road and he could hear the horses' ragged breaths and incoherent rambling from up ahead.

"Haa... haa... how... h-h-how... never will... will... won't accept... not again..."

Thistleman leaned out of the window and he could see the coachman swaying steadily in place, locked in his delirious trance.

It's a miracle the horses haven't collapsed from exhaustion or had a heart attack. I should probably convince the coachman to take a break.

Thistleman attempted to stand up. The shock of all his muscles and nerves crying out in unison knocked him right back down into his seat.

"HEY, COACHMAN! PULL OVER AND TAKE A BREAK!" he managed to bellow.

"Ah... ah, what? Oh, right, yes."

Following orders was baked into the coachman's soul, thankfully more than the horrors he had just witnessed. He pulled over. They had travelled quite far from Kurstwood and were surrounded by farmland. The road quality had improved as they drew closer towards civilization, with occasional hamlets dotting the horizon.

Thistleman steeled his mind, prepared for the pain he knew was coming, and stood up.

"Hrrrrr!!! Ahhhh... It's alright. It's alright. I got this." It had been a *really* long time since he last felt this beat up.

He opened the carriage door and carefully clambered his way to the ground, holding in a groan as he limped his way to the front.

Were carriages always this large?

There it was again. Something was definitely off. Something rather unusual.

"Alright, you are going to rest up here," he said when he got to the coachman. "Get inside the carriage and get some sleep. I will take care of the horses for the night."

It had been nearly two days since the coachman had slept. He just nodded and, with a grunt, curled up in his seat and passed out, without even thinking to question why he was just accepting the direction of such a young boy.

As Thistleman prepared the horses for the night, everything finally started to click.

Were my hands always this small? My arms... are really small too!

In a panic, he started checking everything again.

No wonder everything seemed so large! Is this because of the contract? I know I tried to look more human...but why am I kid? What did I just get myself into?

It was on this frantic musing that Thistleman took watch for the night, cycling between groaning about his injuries and his new predicament.

The coachman snored loudly from the driver's seat while Diane was still passed out and steadily slipping into a calmer rest, allowing the night to pass rather peacefully.

Diane woke to the sound of lively chatter.

She cradled her head in her palm as her stomach yowled with hunger.

"Hauuu..." she groaned to herself. Somehow, in spite of all of this, she felt... stronger. She blinked a few times. Nothing *looked* different, but somehow it all felt... more alive?

Then her latest memories flooded back to her.

The grendel.

Diane flung open the front window of the carriage. "Where! Where is it!?" she screamed in panic.

"Aghhh... watch where you're yelling! Where is what? You are killing my ears!" Thistleman retorted.

Diane blinked again, looking around. Seeing farms and peasants walking along the road and in the fields was a welcome, calming sight. She sighed in relief for a moment before her face paled again. She asked in a shaken voice, "Where... where is everyone else? Hal? Gregory?"

The coachman's face turned dark as he silently shook his head.

Diane bit her lip, desperately stifling her tears to little avail.

"We are getting close to Versailles now. You should probably compose yourself for your report to your father. I'm sure you already know how he is," the coachman said.

Diane nodded. In response to another yowl, Thistleman begrudgingly reached in to the pouch next to him, and pulled out some jerky and crackers.

"Here. Eat this."

A promise is a promise, and mine is as good as law. I agreed to do this stupid contract, so I'll carry it out. And, if I had to hazard a guess from past observations, humans usually don't let their friends starve.

The outer walls of the ducal capital of Versailles slowly inched into view.

Unlike Kurstwood, these walls were made out of stone pulled from nearby quarries. The city was decidedly larger, with nearly one hundred and twenty five thousand residents and another twenty-five thousand in the surrounding rural areas. It was huge even in comparison to most other cities in the kingdom, second only to the royal capital of Archion, and still perhaps larger than many of the cities of the Empire as well.

The wrought-iron gate was raised halfway up into the arched stone of the portcullis, with traffic moving smoothly in and out of the city following quick, cursory inspections by the guards.

As they approached, one of the guards signaled for them to halt.

"Who are you and what is your business here in Versailles today?" she asked in a bored tone.

Diane showed her family crest. "Lady Diane of House Culaine. I am here to see my father."

The guard snickered. "Ah, it's just you? Looks like you're short your usual group. Hah! Well, go on through."

Diane's tightened her fists, but she held in her temper enough to not leap for the prick's throat. "And what would you know of it, hiding here behind the nice city walls? Peons like you are going to be the first to be eaten when the daemons come!" she sniped, shooting a frosty glare as the carriage rolled through the gate. The guard yelled something back, but it was lost in the bustle of the city.

To reach the duke's manor, they just needed to follow the main road past the central market and main trade center. The numerous inns and residential buildings, built with a mix of wood and stone, made way to shops, smithies, tailors, and restaurants. Versailles displayed a level of resplendent wealth that attempted to rival the capital of Archion. Given another hundred years, it could perhaps even become a true rival.

The main roadway was well paved, with trees and flowers lining the center and sides and various parks occasionally breaking up the sprawl. Magical lamps dotted the street, although none were on in the midday sun. No point in wasting the mana crystals, after all.

Within the carriage, Diane sat in silence, staring daggers while Thistleman stared out the window, with a look of complete disinterest on his face. He had found himself in quite a perplexing situation, where he felt he needed to do something for Diane. However, he couldn't recall the last time he had ever been someone's friend. He had no idea what to do.

Sweets?

He imagined getting stabbed for being insensitive.

Wine?

She's a minor! Absolutely not!

A massage?

That was a big NO. He was over ten thousand years old and she was ten! So what if he looked like a kid? Wrong was wrong. Even daemons could have some values and morals, albeit most would be described as severely lacking in that department.

I suspect burning city wouldn't help either. Most humans didn't enjoy the same things he did, so Thistleman pretty much eliminated anything he would do to improve his mood.

Thistleman repressed a sigh. As far as he was concerned, this was the toughest trial he had ever suffered.

Eventually the carriage entered the trade district, which consisted of a huge open field, with numerous paths crisscrossing it. Stalls flanked the pathways, selling all manner of goods. There was a convivial atmosphere, with people drinking and laughing. Some were throwing copper coins into the fountains, for luck, which stood at the convergence of various pathways. Along the outer ring were the major shops — alchemy stores displayed rows of various potions, while magic stores had wands, staves, scrolls, and amulets for sale. Next to them were the armor shops and weapon shops, selling goods produced from the blacksmiths that they had passed by earlier, as well as goods traded with adventurers. In the center of the park stood the three buildings that made up the heart of the city—the Adventurer's Guild Hall, the shrine to Ukemochi, and the Ducal Knight's Garrison. Each had the wealth of the city on full display, and were bustling with activity.

Amongst the various traders, throngs of people were congregating and haggling. From well-dressed nobles wearing flashy outfits heavily adorned with jewelry, with servants and slaves in tow, to mages in all manner and colors of robes, some with large pointy hats, closely followed by their apprentices. There were also the numerous middle-class workers, adventurers, and knights, as well as the countless peasants and street urchins deftly dodging their superiors.

Outside the carriage, people carried on with various conversations and Thistleman listened in.

"What is this weapon? Is it some kind of special stick?" asked an adventurer; curiosity and wonder filled his eyes as he perused the wares of a particularly nice weapon stand.

"Hah! What you are holding is the newest creation of the dwarves! My source wouldn't tell me how he got a hold of it, but he said they call it a Magi-Rifle! You can recharge it by changing out the mana crystal here…" The merchant's face beamed with pride as he strode into making his sales pitch.

"Incredible! It seems no one can match the creativity and skill of the dwarves these days. I hear their cities are an incredible sight to see, like a whole other world!"

"Fortunes! Fortunes! You look like a lucky fellow. Come, I sense a dear family member wants to speak with you!" An elderly old crone waved to a young couple with her gnarled hand, motioning for them to come over.

"What a fraud. Let's just ignore her, dear!" The young woman pulled on the arm of her date.

"Come get the newest delicacy trending in the empire! These candied apples usually sell for five silver, but I am selling them to you today for a mere twenty copper each!" a merchant-chef in a white apron hollered out as a small vat next to him spat out steam.

"I'll take one—hey! Thief! Someone catch that kid, he just stole my wallet! Ani-san, grab me one too, I'll try it after I catch this kid!"

A filthy street urchin dodged out of the crowd, running off just to be plucked up by a nearby guard who confiscated his ill-gotten gains.

"Darrrliiing, you said you are from a rich family, and this amulet would look so good on me, can you pleaaase get it for me?" A noble woman in a garish red dress pouted to her boyfriend in front of a storefront while she pressed herself tightly against him.

"Madame had a wonderful eye, and this amulet is blessed by Inari! I can guarantee if you get it today, you will have many healthy children in the future! Please, come inside and try it on…"

The well-dressed commissionaire ushered the woman with her smitten man inside.

A crier stood upon a small platform with a banner waving behind him. On the banner was a knight kneeling, holding his sword with the tip pointed straight to the ground in front of him, his head lowered, and the full moon rising in the background. To his right of the crier was a table where clerks were filling out rosters as adventurers and down-on-their-luck individuals lined up.

"The goblins, hobgoblins and orcs in the Western Mountains have formed an alliance, but fear not! Great Count Horatio is putting together a subjugation force of talented adventurers, and the church has pledged to support him with their clerics! Food and lodging guaranteed, with a pay of twenty copper per day and a bonus for every slain foe!" the crier called, his voice enhanced by an enchanted megaphone.

"*That* Count Horatio is going? With the church? This mission is practically a guaranteed win!" one armored adventurer spoke to the team with him, sporting a wide and greedy grin.

"This will be the easiest coin I have earned all year! How much is the bonus per head?" the bowman in the group asked.

"Hah, that would be the least of your worries, John. You have enough trouble killing sewer rats." The girl in the robes and pointy hat practically dropped a broadside on their ranger.

"You're one to talk, Beth, you ran away from a small sewer spider!" the flustered ranger shot back, as their party moved to join the line at the tables.

Thistleman's rolled his eyes with disappointment.

Is that really the standard here? Running from small spiders? Seriously?

Chapter 5:
Duke Vermillion

It had taken a little while to navigate past the crowds of the trade district as the sun inched slowly overhead. Compared to the chilliness of the Hawthorne Wilderness, the relatively warm breeze in Versailles was a welcome relief.

The carriage was able to pick up a little more speed as the hubbub thinned out and they entered the noble district. The buildings here were less crowded and larger. Fancy tailors and jewelers sold their wares here as well as high-end restaurants. It was impossible to miss the duke's manor, even amidst all this wealth, as it towered over most of the other buildings. The closer they got to it, the more imposing it seemed. A vast courtyard extended from the main building, filled with gardens and servant houses all intricately designed.

"You know, Hal always said that my fa—that Duke Vermillion built this entire estate just to satisfy his own ego and show off his status. Before him, our family used to live on just a tenth of the land here. He kicked out everyone else that used to live here and bulldozed it all away," Diane murmured dejectedly.

As the carriage slowed to a halt in front of the gates, a pair of well-armed guards in half-plate armor with engraved ceremonial swords at their hips approached them.

"Halt. State your busi—ah, Lady Diane. You have returned from the investigation? I will let the duke know you have arrived."

Diane breathed a sigh of relief to see Gerard, the captain of the guard, manning the gate today. Out of all the duke's guards, he prided himself on his professionalism, and was the only one who didn't call her "the failure" or other names.

"By the way, where—?" Gerard halted mid-sentence, as he saw the pained expression on Diane's face. "Pay no mind. Open the gates!"

The well-oiled gates swung smoothly open.

"Thank you, Gerard. I shall be heading there directly." She gave a curt nod and the carriage resumed its course.

The carriage rattled past numerous pavilions, fountains, ponds, and gardens until it reached the grand entryway to the manor. A series of wide stone stairs led up to the ostentatious wooden doors, currently wide open. Not one of the many bustling servants moved to open the carriage door, instead Diane opened the door herself and hopped out of the carriage.

"Thistleman, come with me. I need you to report to the duke about what happened in Kurstwood!" Diane ordered, as authoritatively as she could.

Really? I am being called like any one of these other pissants? ME?! Well, two can play at the game!

Thistleman leapt into a salute, wielding a giant grin on his face like a weapon as he shouted, "Aye Aye, Boss Lady!"

Diane turned beet red. Not only was the shout excessively loud, but it drew the judgmental stares of all the servants and guards in the vicinity.

"Ah… Just shut up and follow me!" Diane stormed up the steps and through the door. She tried hard to ignore the usual derogatory barrage passed in hushed whispers around the manor.

"Look, the failure is back." a particularly beady-eyed servant jabbed.

"Is it true she was born without magic? What an embarrassment! I bet the duke never hears the end of that one," a visiting minor noble giggled, just within earshot.

"If I was her, I would have already given up. No matter how fancy she tried to make her sword skills, without magic to reinforce them they are just for show." One of the guards shook his head in pity.

"I heard that the Confederation is experiencing a lot of tension amongst the city states, some might declare no confidence to change out the chairman. Do you think that could be useful?" one adjutant asked another man.

"If that's the case, maybe the duke can send Diane to network in one of their lesser households! If another factional skirmish breaks out there, she would certainly be tied in with the losing side and, with her lack of magic, we would finally be rid of her," a well-dressed advisor interjected.

"We could also send her to serve the Empire's church in Dyrrachion. I heard that the church has denounced Emperor Hirihito, so if tensions boil over there, she would almost certainly bite it!"

Diane approached the hall where the duke normally carried out his daily duties. Thistleman followed closely behind her, eyeing each and every servant and attendant. *Their casual cruelty is hardly any different than that of daemons,* he mused. However, the problem was that in looking down on her, they were also looking down on him.

In time, you will all suffer. I will find a way, you have my word! AND I WILL HAVE THIS WORLD COME TO FEAR US, JUST AS ALL THOSE FOOLS WHO CAME BEFORE YOU FEARED ME. Us? Yes, Diane too. To be called my master and friend, I will accept no less. She will need to learn to stand on the same stage as I.

A malicious, hideous grin snaked across Thistleman's face. It managed to rip all the attention away from Diane, causing the servants surrounding them to immediately hush and recoil. There was one that looked especially shocked, that damnable advisor who wanted to ship Diane off to die. The man exuded arrogance and had a sigil of a knight kneeling with his sword before the rising moon etched onto the left breast of his pompous jacket.

Diane spied the reaction from those gathered in the hall, but before she could spot the source of their dismay, Thistleman assumed a neutral expression, offering a simple shrug to her concerned glance.

"Ignore the servants," she said. "They don't matter. Don't listen to them. Don't react to them. You belong to me and I am all that matters! Since you are mine that means you have worth, you must pay them no mind!"

"Yes, my lady! You are absolutely correct, my lady! Please forgive this one, my lady!"

Nailed it!

Diane's face turned red. "I... I... focus on your report! The duke is on the other side of this door! And make sure to treat him with courtesy and respect." She spun around, shoving the doors with all her might.

The knight stood in the center of the room wearing full plate armor. His adamantium claymore was strapped firmly to his back, angled to allow for it to be easily unsheathed. On the left side of his chest plate he sported a sigil of a golden shield, and within the shield's borders two red lions circled an ornate scepter.

A red carpet ran from the center of the room to the head, where a throne of hewn rock sat. Large purple and gold banners decorated the walls behind it.

One of the four pillars of the Kingdom of Luthas, Duke Vermillion made sure his power was fully on display. His deceptively simple outfit was designed to emphasize his physique, highlighting his broad shoulders and toned muscles rippling through his tight sleeves. His large stature and powerful, square jaw ensured a completely intimidating package.

His cold blue eyes betrayed no emotion, although when settling upon Diane, he could not hide his disdain. To his right, an aide shuffled through papers at a table, sorting page after page full of notes on the duke's decisions throughout the day that needed to be turned into the appropriate laws and decrees.

"Duke Vermillion, as we have already spoken at length and concluded the majority of our business, I shall allow our guest here a moment before we finish up. I suppose such an... audacious entrance must be due to something important." The knight stepped humbly aside to a corner of the chamber.

The duke nodded for Diane to come forward; the disdain turned to fury in his eyes.

"So, for what reason have you come to so boldly interrupt my meeting with the emissary from our esteemed imperial neighbors and waste the lieutenant's valuable time?" The duke didn't spare an ounce of hostility as he addressed Diane.

Diane walked as proudly as she could manage to the center of the room, attempting to fulfill every expected courtesy as she knelt before her father.

Thistleman, however, didn't move a step past the door. Instead, he stood with his arms crossed, offering nothing but a look of passive disinterest, as if he was staring at an insignificant inferior being.

It seemed the Duke hadn't noticed the blatant slight yet due to his focus on Diane. However, Lieutenant Septimus caught it immediately. A small smile escaped his lips. *Either that child is suicidal, or he has balls tougher than steel. Perhaps a bit of both?* If this wasn't a foreign kingdom, and he wasn't in the audience chamber of one of their most influential lords, he would have inducted that brat into the Imperial Knight Order one way or another. *Mad bastards like him make some of the best knights, after all.* Septimus gave up his grin for the moment. No use dreaming about what he couldn't have.

Diane's eyes were pointed straight down, and she didn't dare to look up. Her small body was trembling.

"Fath—" she began.

"That is Duke Vermillion to you. Speak quickly!"

"Duke Vermillion, per your orders, I took my knights and mage to investigate the loss of contact with Kurstwood, the village you assigned to me.

However, when we arrived there... we found the village had been completely destroyed. While we were investigating, we were attacked by a demon. Everyone... everyone who came with me, they all died. I am not sure how we survived but we managed to escape from it."

Duke Vermillion realized that he now had a new opportunity to deal with this stain on his family's reputation. Failure to protect one's domain through negligence was considered a capital offense. He hid his malicious glee behind a façade of anger.

"So, you interrupted my meeting with the Imperial Knights' lieutenant to tell me you allowed your village, the one I entrusted to you, to be destroyed, and you managed to get all your knights killed in the process? And that the most information you could bring to me is that it was some demon who did it? The Demon Lord's empire is on the other side of the ocean! There is no way he came all the way from Ebenheim, ignored the Empire of the Sand, and laid waste to one of our villages! You cannot even properly identify the difference between a daemon and a demon! And now you come back here in such disgrace, foisting responsibility onto us to right your failures? Such a pathetic showing cannot be tolerated in our family!"

Giving Diane Kurstwood as her only holding had been the right decision. A village so close to the wilderness was bound to get destroyed or raided, especially if he never provided any support. Although he had hoped such a raid would take Diane down with it, at least this much was enough.

"Diane, you have disgraced our kingdom and have proven your incompetence! You do not deserve to be called a noble, and are nothing but a hindrance to any who would serve under you. For the good of the kingdom, I retract your status as a noble and banish you from House Culaine! Begone!"

If I could spread my influence even into the empire, perhaps I could get enough backing to replace our pathetic king too. The Kingdom needs a strong leader, and if I could command the respect of even the Empire, then I can contend even with the archdukes to succeed the king!

Duke Vermillion's self-satisfaction quickly waned, as instead of a look of approval from Lieutenant Septimus, the knight's gaze was directed at the young boy scowling near the door at the back of the throne room. That peasant was staring at him with clear hatred! The duke blanched as the boy turned his back on him. Diane, tears pouring down her face, grabbed Thistleman's hand and dragged him through the door.

I am Duke Vermillion, and I will not stand for a peasant to look down upon me like this!

With a deft flick of his wrist, the duke launched a poisoned blade out of a concealed sheath at incredible speed towards Thistleman. While publicly killing his daughter would be considered unacceptable, nobody would care if he killed a peasant who insulted him. However, the dagger never made contact. Instead, it seemed to miss his head by mere millimeters, and struck his advisor square in the neck.

The duke stood, flabbergasted. He never missed! Then he saw who he had struck.

The person he just killed would bring a lot of trouble indeed, as it was none other than the fourth son of Count Horatio. This blunder would bring far too much trouble, and he needed to find an excuse quickly!

Perhaps if I pin the blame on that peasant as an assassin, and killed him before anyone could prove otherwise... that would work!

However, before he could speak...

"Duke Vermillion, as it seems you are more interested in petty disputes and killing those within your own halls who displease you rather than deal with *clear and active threats to your kingdom and domain*, I suppose we have nothing left to discuss here. In the empire, we do try to maintain a somewhat higher level of civility. As this issue pertains to my mission here, and with your king's permission, we will be heading north to Kurstwood in your stead. I pray you will show more restraint with your subjects in the future."

Lieutenant Septimus graced the Duke with a curt nod, before marching out of the chamber himself.

The damage was done. Vermillion swore to remember the face of that peasant. He was not known as one of the pillars of the Kingdom for nothing, and once things got settled with Count Horatio—which knowing him, would likely take a very long time—he would punish Diane and that peasant *properly*.

Diane sprinted out of the manor as fast as her little legs were able, dragging Thistleman behind her. She needed to leave here as fast as possible, and her father was clearly in a killing mood. He had killed Asimore!

She spotted the coachman with her carriage parked alongside a magnificent carriage of black, gold, and red. It was likely that distinguished knight's carriage, and was heavily guarded by other resplendent knights. Not that it mattered to her at this moment.

"Hey Coachman, we need to leave, now!" she shouted with utmost urgency.

"Aieee, what is the hurry little miss? We just got here. This old man needs his rest and I am not about to go out on another one of your dangerous ventures!"

"The duke just banished me and killed Asimore!"

"What?!? Damnit! This is trouble indeed!"

He knew his career working for House Culaine was over. The duke would likely vent his anger by killing anyone closely associated with Diane, and if he couldn't kill them, he would pressure them and ruin their lives with ruthless efficiency. Although to make such a mistake as killing Asimore.... In his long years working for the Culaine family, that was most unlike the duke.

"Hyah, time to move again yeh lazy horses!" The horses begrudgingly began to trot around the fountain and back onto the road out of the estate. "I have family in the port city of Njord, and that is part of the king's territory. I can take you there and while I certainly won't risk harboring you, we will at least be safe from his immediate reach."

"Thanks... and... I am sorry, but I never did ask for your name," Diane caught her breath as she spoke, her heart still racing.

"Don't worry about it. In fact, I would be just fine if you kept calling me Coachman. The saving grace of peasants like us is that if nobody ever cared to learn our names, then it makes hiding away from aggrieved lords all the easier." The coachman smiled a large, toothy grin as the carriage hurriedly left the estate.

"So, Diane... are you going to ever let go of my hand?" Thistleman prodded her.

The fact she was still holding Thistleman's hand after running with him all the way through the manor and into the carriage suddenly came into sharp focus. Her face turned so red that even the red sheen of the reddest apples could not compare to its radiance. She made a sound so unladylike at that moment that she swore Thistleman to secrecy on it for the rest of his life.

Chapter 6:
Ambush

Gus stood on a small rock ledge near the main road into Njord, perhaps a day's ride out from the city.

The ends of his golden-blond hair bounced from his broad shoulders as he walked towards the edge of a short cliff, dancing in the breeze along with the ragtag fur mixed in with pieces of leather armor. His protective wear was lacking as he didn't have enough to cover all his vital areas, leaving most of his stomach exposed, revealing a well-defined core.

By his side he carried an iron long sword, which unlike the rest of his gear was probably the only thing worth any proper value.

He pulled a small brooch out of his pocket, fondly touching the picture stored inside. It was an old family picture from when he was a young child with his baby sister plopped square in his lap, and his mother and father standing behind them.

"Don't worry Nina, even with Mom and Dad gone... after I do this job, I will be able to take care of you. I won't have to do work like this anymore," Gus whispered.

Life at the edge of the wilderness was a hard one. Adventurers who tried to venture into the uncivilized parts of the world faced death, dismemberment, or worse on a regular basis. Military life was not much better, if you didn't have the means to be anything other than fodder.

If you couldn't land a good trade apprenticeship or get into work for one of the noble houses, then you were left to struggle relentlessly at any of the myriad hard labor jobs for barely enough money to live on.

Just a little more and we can move to somewhere quiet and warm. We'll be able to buy a cozy little tavern to work and live in!

"Hey boss, we just got word from our lookout. The carriage is coming through and it perfectly matches the description. We are gonna be rich with this one!"

A beautiful girl jogged out from the trees behind Gus, longbow in hand. She wore fur armor intentionally cut out at the midriff, the calf sections, and part of the chest piece, revealing her ample cleavage.

"Amala, I still can't stand what you did to that armor we made for you. Do you know how hard it was to hunt a dire wolf and get an undamaged piece of its hide?" Gus lamented, his mouth curled in dismay as he looked upon the results of her handiwork.

"Oh come on, boss, you have to admit nobody questions a pretty girl even if she is selling stolen goods! Plus, it makes the guys drop their guard and we get so many better deals!" Amala leaned in seductively, squeezing just enough with her arms to accentuate her form.

Damn manipulative witch! Gus averted his eyes, attempting to hide a slight rush of blood to his cheeks as he did so.

"Anyways, we can deal with this later," he continued after an uncomfortable silence. "Let's move into position. Tell the lookouts to slip in and ambush them from behind."

"Hmph. Fine." Amala pouted.

It had been a little over a week since they left Versailles.

The carriage ride had been a quiet one as they avoided staying in any of the settlements and villages in case of any danger within the duke's territory. The fewer people that saw them, the better. Still, with a carriage as notable as Diane's, as she was still the daughter of the Duke, they had been quite fortunate so far.

Thistleman was utterly perplexed at the situation. Not only could he see the distress and worry on Diane and the coachman's face, but he could also feel the pain Diane was holding in. It seemed to him that she was just trying to put up a strong front.

I get that we are all too weak right now to properly deal with this but still, running away and hiding like this just feels so absolutely wrong.

He watched a slow and steady drip of mana flow into the silent girl's mana heart, pulling in just as much as it needed to grow like a thirsty seedling that finally reached water. Stunted, weak, and yet still unwilling to give up.

Thistleman scrunched his face as he scanned the forest once again, failing to hide his disgust as he noticed someone watching them, hidden within the tree line just beyond the supposed border of the dukedom. He sharpened the mana in his eyes.

Detect Life.

A pair of watchers to cut off our retreat... and three more people ahead.

Thistleman seethed. *The balls on these pissants. Predictable, stupid, and all too common.*

"Bandits ahead! Hold on tight, I'm turning us around n—keugh!" The coachman's yell was cut off as an arrow pierced his throat.

The carriage lost control and veered to the side, with the crack and crash of one of the wheels shattering against a large rock and the snap of the horses' bridles. The horses whinnied loudly as they dashed into the trees.

Diane screamed, her shrieking continued until the carriage finally came to an abrupt halt. "No no no no no, not now! Why? Why can't he leave me be? What am I supposed to do? Just leave me alone!" She tried to curl into a corner of the carriage.

Thistleman grabbed Diane's arm firmly, and with his other hand forced her to look straight into his eyes, even while tears streamed down her face.

"Diane, breathe! You still have your rapier. You are only dead if you give up now! The first bandit is coming for the door, so don't stop to think about it. As soon as he opens the door, pierce his throat, and clear the two behind the carriage. I will distract the bandits up front!"

Something in his eyes was... mesmerizing. A calm began to fill her and the fear felt like it was fading. In its place... rage. Lines of energy began to form over Diane's heart and across Thistleman's right hand, dark lines that quickly began to glow. The sigils that should have formed when the contract was first formed finally began to emerge. As Thistleman felt her emotions, his emotions also flowed into her. His rage *was* her rage.

Fear and pain shall be repaid in ash and death!

Then the door opened with a horrifically slow creak, almost as if time itself slowed down.

So far, so good.

Her shot was perfect and the coachman was down, and now it was just a couple of little kids. Putting them down would be the easiest money she'd ever made! *A magicless little girl and a peasant, at that!*

A smile enveloped her face, although she quickly hid it when she noticed the serious look on Gus's face.

Why can't he just have fun with it like the rest of us? Amala pouted as she notched another arrow. *I'll show him how to really have some fun!*

The other bandits whooped in excitement, rushing towards the undefended carriage. The first to the carriage door was a gangly fellow with a freakish smile, revealing many missing and rotten teeth.

However, their joy was short lived. The door was flung aside as a ball of unfettered rage screeched out with reckless abandon. The bandit couldn't react in time as the blade came for him, held by a small girl whose face was twisted with anger. The tip of the weapon pierced through the gangly man's eye and into his skull. The girl twisted her body around to use his shoulders as a launching pad, the blade tearing free from his skull, spilling grey matter as Diane dashed towards the bandits in the rear.

She was followed by a disheveled looking boy who leapt out of the carriage and, seemingly without surveying a single thing around him, dashed straight towards Amala.

"Damnit! You should've just accepted your death, you fucking kids!" Amala screamed, loosing her arrow. An odd drop-step by the boy caused the arrow to fly just over his shoulder.

"Don't get distracted by rage, Amala! The boy is unarmed, he is probably just trying to buy her time. The girl is the main target. Leave no witnesses and I will get the girl!" Gus grimaced, then dashed past the boy as Amala readied another arrow.

She shot... and she missed.

She aimed and shot again, sure that this time it would hit the boy's chest, just as the arrow skimmed over his other shoulder.

"You think getting behind me will help you?! Stupid brat!" Her voice shook with anger.

She shot again, missing for a fourth time.

"This damn bow must be broken. You think you can run from me?!" Amala dropped her bow, pulled out her dagger, and began to chase the boy as he turned and beelined straight towards the other side of the forest.

Thistleman tried desperately to hide his maliciously satisfied smile. Those arrogant idiots were playing straight into his hands.

If that archer and swordsman were to focus on Diane, their combination would be too much for her too handle. So the answer was obvious, he just needed to split them up. He glanced behind him–the two lookouts behind the carriage were already dead, one blow each.

Gus seemed shocked at the girl's blind ferocity and was barely holding on, dripping with blood. Even while blocking any strikes coming for his exposed stomach, her blade found its way into the other exposed parts of his body. Between her small size and improved speed, his large blade would never be able to easily reach her on its own.

Oh? What's this? Thistleman's eyes darted a little deeper in the woods, spotting the mana outline of a creature. A huge smile stretched across his face! A purely innocent smile. Purely. Innocent.

Amala was absolutely focused on Thistleman.

She would never hear the end of it from the others if she couldn't even kill one kid! She kept chasing him deeper into the woods, ducking through the trees and pressing on through the rapidly thickening brush. She was breathing heavily and her hair was thoroughly messed up.

"What the hell is up with these kids? This was supposed to be easy money! Shouldn't I be laughing my way back to the camp already!?" Amala grunted fiercely, as she had to yank her hair out of yet another branch.

Thistleman cut around a large tree up ahead and as she came around the corner, she ran face first into something large and very furry. She fell ass-backwards, cursing before the blood drained from her face. The boy was nowhere to be seen but the creature in front of her turned and glowered at her, blood dripping from its fangs. The carcass of a wild boar, partially eaten, lay behind it.

No no no! Where's the kid? Shouldn't he have run into it first?

Amala recognized it immediately, just as it seemed to tilt its head in acknowledgement of the fur she was wearing. She crawled backwards away from the dire wolf as fast as she could without turning her back towards it for a second.

Thistleman savored her scream as he made his way back to the carriage.

It's a shame I can't watch.

Thistleman sighed. Sneaking around and manipulating things like this was certainly not his strong suit, especially when compared to other daemons. Or demons, now? Still, it was a relief that even with his reserves of mana so low, he was able to shadow step from the sight of these pathetic creatures. Silver linings and all.

If I could actually do all the fighting myself then this would all have been just a joke.

His rage at these creatures began to subside. They were just a bothersome waste of his time, inconveniencing him while dying for nothing at all.

Hopefully this world will have someone who can offer me a worthwhile challenge.

Diane had never moved this quickly nor felt this strong in her life. From the moment the door opened, it felt as if she had been in a non-stop rush. After leaping off the corpse of the first bandit, she rushed to the closest one behind the carriage. She saw him raise his bow, and it all felt so incredibly slow. She could watch precisely where the arrow was aimed.

Diane dodged to the right. The arrow missed completely.

She could see the fear in the bandit's eyes. The rush was taking over. She saw an opening in his neck-guard and stabbed straight through his throat.

She pulled her blade out deftly and dodged around the falling corpse, dashing to the next bandit.

He turned to run, but not fast enough. She leapt onto his back and stabbed him through the ear.

You will never try to take from me again!

She felt almost... *liberated* with the overflowing rage, venting out her years of abuse, pain, and suffering. She didn't even notice she was laughing as the blood rained onto her.

She turned to look at Gus like a blood-soaked little devil. He was charging towards her much too late.

His face was perfectly calm, though there was a slight tremble in his hands.

Diane was thoroughly unaware of how terrifying she looked appeared.

Gus strained his eyes and attempted to concentrate some mana into them as he stared at Diane.

A monster worse than a damn dire wolf. How the hell did anyone mistake her as inept? Is this a setup for the duke to get rid of us?

Gus panicked at the thought, and he knew he would need Amala's help if he was going to kill the girl.

She moved after him quickly, her blade aimed straight for his face. He used his longsword to deflect the rapier, but she struck quickly.

He dodged as best he could, but cuts were rapidly appearing on the unprotected parts of his body. He was losing blood quickly. Gus tried a counter-swing , but she was so short she easily dodged under his arm and his blade only hit earth. Then he felt a searing pain in his calf.

Gus despised his lack of talent. It was what had forced him into this life in the first place.

He swung his blade low, sweeping behind himself and forcing Diane to leap back.

Taking the opportunity to breathe, Gus yelled, "Amala, where are you? Stop playing around. I need help here now!"

He looked around quickly but she was nowhere to be seen. Nor was the peasant boy. Dread filled him.

I'm going to die here.

"I'm sorry, Nina," Gus whispered as he let the sword fall from his hands, succumbing to despair. His sight went black as the rapier pierced up through his chin.

Diane was breathing heavily, steam wafting from her body. The rush faded along with the rage. Exhaustion seeped into every pore.

She heard the patter of feet running and stopping further down the road to see a lookout they had missed.

Diane's surprise was met with an expression of terror on his face as he realized everyone else was dead. He naturally wasted no time as he turned to flee.

"Damnit! *Fireball!*"

It was nowhere near as powerful as when she was forcefully awakened as she had less mana to draw on. However, the raging flames flew true down the road and exploded on contact with the back of the bandit. He screamed in agony and Diane shuddered as the rage finally left her. She looked at the blood dripping from her hands and the corpses left in her wake.

I... did all this?

Her vision grew blurry as she heaved the contents of her stomach onto the side of the road.

"Hey Diane, I think I lost her. Do you think you can find the horses? They shouldn't have run far, I will grab our supplies and get us out of here! Hey, Diane? You listening?" Thistleman prodded, carefully looking for any wounds on her.

Ah, right. Some humans get a little strange about killing each other. I need to break that attitude before it causes some serious problems.

"W-what? Oh, y-yeah, you're right. Don't take long, I'll be right back!" Diane stuttered in surprise, before looking into the woods. She spotted where the horses had charged through the brush and followed the trail they blazed.

Seems that got her mind back in order for now... although, there is another odd feeling there?

There *was* some kind of emotion there, but unlike the others, it felt just out of his reach.

Thistleman took stock of the bodies, counting to make sure no one was missed and looting anything valuable along the way. He found some odd looking tokens on them.

Considering their line of work, it's probably some identifier that they use. I bet there's a high chance it helps them find people to sell-off their stolen goods to.

Thistleman's eyebrow twitched at a new thought. *This means they were at least professional enough to be hired. By the Duke? Perhaps... a last minute attempt at revenge? Someone of his wealth certainly should have been able to afford better...*

Thistleman paced slowly and pensively toward the last bandit Diane had killed. *Ah, right. Seems everyone was worked up about that Horatio guy. He probably needed to keep his best cards for that fight.*

When he was searching Gus, he found the locket with a picture in it. He looked it over carefully, judging the picture with a furrowed brow. Diane came running up behind him, having picked up the horses who hadn't run far.

"I got them. Let's go! Hey, whatcha looking at?"

If she really is one of those sensitive humans then the picture might break her mind.

Down went the brooch.

"I found a great snack! This guy had a sweet muffin on him! It was delicious." Innocent. Absolutely innocent! Thistle went for a dumb smile.

"You found a snack and didn't share? Greedy! Why am I having to be so nice to you?" Diane smacked him on the side of his head in a huff.

"I'm sorry! I didn't know you would want some! I will give you the next one! I promise!"

"I did all the work so everything here is mine! How can you give me what is already mine?"

They continued arguing like this as they mounted the horses and quickly made their way to the port city of Njord.

Chapter 7:
Port City of Njord

Badump.

Something... felt strange.

Where, or what... is this place?

I felt as if I were watching the world through someone else's eyes, unable to move my own hands and feet.

Badump.

Everything felt a little... blurry. I was inside someone's home; that much was obvious. A mostly bare place, with some scattered junk, likely the kind of trinkets humans loved to have. At least it was clean, with wooden plank walls and a stone fireplace with a small cauldron filled with some kind of stew. I couldn't stop myself as I walked to the pot and used a wooden ladle to fill a wooden bowl with the stew.

I carried that bowl of stew to what looked like the only bed in the home, where a woman lay with a crying newborn babe, while a tall man held her hands. They smiled at me though their faces were blurry.

Badump.

The world shifted and the woman changed. She wailed as tears stained her cheeks and her eyes rolled back into her head. She was completely emaciated and this time everything was clear. Black spots and pustules covered her body. Her gnarled hands reached out towards… us?

Why am I holding the young babe?

Badump.

The world shifted yet again. There was a cleric standing nearby and a tall man whose lips were twisted with grief. I watched the woman's corpse burn in a dirt hole before it was buried beneath the earth.

Badump.

These were clearly someone's memories, but whose?

The tall man's bluish lips and cracked neck greeted me this time. He dangled limply from a rope hung from a ceiling beam, the stool he'd stood upon knocked aside.

The fragility of humans never ceases to amaze me. How could a single species vary to such extremes?

Badump.

The world shifted again and an angry-looking man ran past me. I was cowering with a child; we were clearly hiding from him. As she whimpered in hunger, I pulled out a neatly wrapped slice of bread from a pocket. She looked emaciated with hunger.

Badump.

"—thistle" A whisper pierced my consciousness and there was a slight pressure on my shoulder.

"HEY THISTLEMAN!" Diane shouted.

I practically fell off the horse as my eyes snapped open.

Good. At least that's over with.

"Finally, you're awake. You had me worried, spacing out like that! So don't do that anymore, 'kay?"

How am I supposed to not do something that I don't know I'm doing in the first place?

"I'm sorry... I'll see what I can do about it." I shrugged with a somewhat pained and confused expression.

Now that I really think about it, all those people I saw, weren't they the ones from the locket?

"Its fine, don't worry about it. We are about to reach the gate, so just follow my lead."

At least she adjusts pretty quickly. Resilient kid.

I wasn't in a particular rush, but I figured I would have time to investigate this locket issue later.

The sky was overcast as they approached Njord. Massive wooden walls surrounded the city, each post in the wall looked like someone had just planted a whole tree and lopped off the top.

Rumor had it, the city itself was first founded thirteen-hundred years ago by a man claiming to be a powerful Viking lord from a world completely unlike their own. While most believed the truth behind its founder was likely exaggerated or embellished, none could contest he established one of the most fearsome raiding fleets of his era and terrorized much of the coast of Anastasia. After his death, his many children picked up his mantle, but due to constant infighting, the city never grew to be much larger than it was today. The city maintained its way of life until three-hundred years ago when Luthas the Great began his wars of unification. The city, weakened by a millennia of infighting, submitted to Luthas when his armies marched north, sparing them from destruction and allowing them to maintain their traditions in exchange for their loyalty.

As such, the men of Njord swore their loyalty to the king and his direct heirs. Luthas had granted the city a certain level of autonomy to maintain a peaceful balance, which helped it to become one of the fastest growing cities in the kingdom. The city was led by a chief minister elected by the people with the region being managed by a baron appointed by the king, directly from the noble families of Njord. This resulted in Njord being the farthest reach of royal land from the capital and one of the king's most powerful backers. It also made the direct political influence of the other lords and ladies of the land extremely weak.

Numerous long houses filled the city, built with a mix of wood and clay. The roofs were covered with thatch, with the wealthier houses and shops replacing much of the thatch with wooden slats and clay tiles. The powerful nobles' homes and the churches stood several stories high, adorned with various carvings of large sea serpents, carnivorous fish, and krakens.

Half the city was built out on to the ocean itself, protected from the waves by a large stone seawall with an entry gate for ships entering the port and fisherman leaving the city. Most settlements near the wilderness were eventually ravaged and destroyed by the monsters and demi-humans who would occasionally go out on raids. The survival and growth of this city was a testament to the hardiness of its people.

"HALT! State your business in Njord, travelers!" a male guard commanded in a stern Njordic accent.

A large, burly man with blue eyes and blond hair marched forward to address Diane and Thistleman as they arrived. He wore well-maintained fur armor, and his arm rested calmly on his sheathed sword, likely made of cold iron, a specialty in the region said to rival steel mainly due to its effectiveness and durability against monsters, although far weaker when used in dealing with people.

The two children stopped their horses, the pitiful creatures snorted and shook their manes, thankful for a break.

Before Diane could answer, a female guard stepped forward and chastised the man.

"Bjorn, give these kids a break. Just look at them and the condition they are in! Come now, you're safe from any trouble here."

The woman had a slim build but was more defined than the man, and she had a large scar cutting across her face. Instead of furs, she wore a cold iron chain shirt over leather armor and a cold iron helmet with fur ear guards. She used her long silver spear as a walking stick; the soft thuds of its base hitting the ground became clearer as she approached. Her long blond hair was curled in to a bun behind her head, and her silver eyes shone with a kind expression.

"My name is Brunhilde, please forgive Bjorn for his stiffness. He is a new guard here and I am overseeing his training. Now, I know this may be hard for you, but please tell me about what troubles brought you here in such a manner?" Brunhilde emanated a disarming demeanor, and she asked her question while reaching up to pat Diane on the head. Meanwhile, Bjorn's face winced at the critique, but he quickly resumed his stoic behavior.

"My name is Diane. Diane Culaine. I was coming here with my... servant, Thistleman, and our coachman when we were assaulted by bandits. I... I managed to kill most of them before we were able to flee. I don't know if there are any more. Also, can you please stop patting my head? I'm not a kid!"

"Wait... you were assaulted by bandits? And you both killed them?" Brunhilde's eyes widened, as she looked between the two disheveled kids.

"No, *she* killed them. I only ran around. Oh, and here, they had these tokens on them!" Thistleman chimed in, and tried to pass over the tokens to the guards.

He had smiled quite pleasantly at Brunhilde, or so he thought, but the fact he talked about killing people so nonchalantly really threw her off. Diane's pained reaction made sense, even if the fact of the kid killing bandits did not. But Thistleman... that cold, emotionless smile just gave her the chills.

"No... you should keep those to turn in to the Adventurer's Guild. Those are Thieves' Guild tokens and you will be able to claim a reward for turning them in. Also... are you *sure* you were the ones who killed the bandits? How many of them were there? Ah... wait, never mind."

Brunhilde quickly changed her line of questioning as Diane tightened her fists on her horse's reigns, her eyes boring holes into her.

"Just... let us see your identification then, and you can head on over to the guild."

In response, Diane pointed at the crest on her bloodstained dress.

"This is all the identification I have with me."

Brunhilde sighed. She looked carefully at the crest, and nodded. "House Culaine. Well, it will have to do. When you head into the city, make sure you swing by the city's government office for new entry permits. An adventurer's card works just as well, but I think you are a bit young to get one of those.

"Also, try to avoid the Brahmoun District. That area can be quite seedy and wouldn't be safe for you kid," Bjorn chimed in, trying to sound useful.

"Thanks, we will try and take your advice," Diane responded, trying to regain her noble bearing before riding into the city. They could hear Brunhilde chiding Bjorn again about not scaring kids as they rode deeper in to the city, although this time with notably less energy than before.

Diane and Thistleman rode slowly through the city. Diane's exhaustion was starting to catch up with her, but she remained focused and continued looking for the Adventurer's Guild.

Thistleman acted as if he was tired as well, even though daemons weren't particularly known to need sleep. Still, he had to play his part. Even if it was a... peasant's role. However, Sen—*Thistleman* never failed at anything. If he was to be a peasant supporting Diane, his "bestest" friend, then that meant he would be the best damn peasant friend she'd ever had! As a best friend, he would be just as tired as her, and persevere just as long! Except he wasn't tired. At all. He tried not to think about that part.

At least trying to figure out how to fulfill his new role was absolutely fascinating, particularly because it involved concepts so absolutely *foreign* to him. He'd had ten thousand years of study on annihilating things, all things, everything. He was probably the foremost expert on the topic in the multiverse. But... how the hell did being a friend work?

The city had a very different vibe than Versailles. Other than the architecture, the people themselves behaved vastly differently. There seemed to be less entitlement and a stronger focus on community than business amongst the residents. People were also notably much poorer than in the ducal capital. And more heavily armed. Probably due to cultural traditions and living on the edge of a violent wilderness?

Eventually, the pair reached the Adventurer's Guild. It was located at the last patch of shoreline before the road was replaced by wood-plank pathways, expertly built to rise and fall with the water and preserved with magic. The pathways connected all the different buildings and districts out on the water. Kids could be seen diving off some of the buildings into the water, clearly undeterred by the colder temperatures. Some of the sections had old men sitting in chairs, with their rods in hand and a line in the water. Others had bridges between sections, and people paddling around them in small boats... for fun?

Diane didn't bother to look around as she quietly plodded onward. She was here for the Adventurer's Guild, and she would need to collect the money so she could get a place to sleep.

Get in the guild. Get some money. Find an inn... then... find work? People usually just give us money... so who gives them their money?

They dismounted and hitched their horses by the water trough near the guild. The horses were all too happy to finally have a break, and slurped up the water ferociously before nodding off at the first opportunity.

Diane hauled herself up the small set of stairs that led to the front porch of the guild, covered with a nice plank roof. The double doors were made of a solid dark oak, with a deep red border around them and golden handles. On one door was a large gold plate with the image of the known world, Anastasia and Ebenheim, surrounded by a great serpent, known locally as Jormungand, the World Eater. This was the crest of the Njord branch of the Adventurer's Guild.

As Diane started reaching for the handle of one of the enormous doors, it was jolted inward. A group of rough looking individuals barreled out, not paying any attention to Diane or Thistleman as they sauntered past. The inside of the guild was noisy. Apparently, a lot was happening around the world.

Various adventuring and mercenary groups gathered around tables with flagons of ale, debating and arguing over posted requests and hearsay.

A large band of mercenaries boisterously bantered over a new posting that had found its way to their table, with only criers recruiting for other missions able to shout above them.

"Have you heard? The Frost Queen has declared war on the dwarves of Moeria again. Seems they weren't prepared this time. They have posted some pretty hefty mercenary recruitment ads." A balding, steel clad man with glasses stared at the posting, while nudging a stout bearded fellow in the seat next to him.

"How hefty? I hear those snow elves are an extremely violent lot. If you don't die by their hands, living as their slaves is arguably much worse..." The bearded man grunted thickly, guzzling an entire pint to himself.

"Five hundred gold coins for participating, and a dwarven crafted weapon if you do especially well." The entire table lit up like a beehive.

"Damn, they are desperate to offer that much! But... to get my hands on a dwarven weapon? I think it might be worth the risk." A dark cloaked man on the other side of the table tossed a particularly keen dagger in the air and caught it again, smiling with a hint of greed.

"Plus, I hear that Frost Queen is quite the beauty. I wouldn't mind dying if it's by her hands." A younger lad, barely a day over seventeen gawked over the bald man's shoulder.

"This is why you never get any girls. You really need to stop coming off as so desperate!" Another young lad jabbed his elbow into the side of the first kid, while his eyes wandered over the poster all the same.

"Philistander's Hunters are currently looking for a healer! We are hunting the mighty sabretooth, and promise an equal share in the reward!" A well-dressed ranger leapt atop a table, his green hood pulled black while his cloak swished elegantly behind him.

"How would we even get down there? I hear piracy has gotten even worse in the Treacherous Isles, and the land route is so far the war might be over by the time we reach there." Another bald mercenary slammed his flagon onto the table and leaned in incredulously.

"That is a fair problem, but it can also be a boon. I hear there is also an extra reward for capturing pirate bounties. We can make a quick buck on the way to our next job!" the glasses-wearing man responded, as he leafed through a few other pamphlets.

"Hahaha, now that is thinking with your noggin!" The bearded man laughed heartily.

"Captain Morgan is looking for several groups of adventurers to provide security for his ship on a voyage to the Empire of the Sand. Meals will be provided, as it is a round-trip we are willing to accept adventurers for security on one or both directions." A well-dressed sailor with a particularly nice feathered hat contrasting his rough features shouted well above the din as he read off his announcement, much to the chagrin of the ranger.

He ignored the scowls from the green-cloaked man, as a pair of men in clerical robes patted the ranger on shoulder before walking over to speak with the feathered-hat crier.

"A lot of other adventurers are also heading south, but I hear it is for different mercenary jobs. Some other groups still in the kingdom are hiring adventurers left and right," the only canian in the group barked, his dog-like snout dripped with froth from his mug.

"Yeah, it seems they are paying well enough and there is no fighting involved. Definitely a lot safer than hunting monsters up here." One of the youths jumped back in excitedly.

"That crier for Captain Morgan sounds pretty interesting. I always wanted to visit the Empire of the Sand. I don't trust a damned soul who recruits adventurers and mercs for 'peaceful jobs', but I hear the drow are pretty close to the humans up there. I also know from very reliable sources that they are much better to deal with than the snow elves! I say we check up on that job instead, eh boys?" the bearded man demurred.

As he stood up to go speak with the feather-hatted man, he yelled out to one of the serving girls, "Aye, lassie! Another round for me boys over 'ere!"

Diane and Thistleman made their way through the crowd of adventurers to the front desk, occasionally dodging a spilled drink and the feet of heavily armored paladins and knights. They arrived just as a man in full-plate mail armor picked up a small purse of gold from the attendant and walked away.

"Next! Nyah!" A fuzzy catkin called out to the group. She had silk black fur, round cat-like eyes, and pointy cat ears. Long whiskers poked out from a small patch of white fur around her nose, and a pair of small, sharp teeth protruded from her mouth. She was absolutely adorable.

"NYEXT!" she called out again. Someone behind Diane and Thistleman pointed down to the two kids at the foot of the counter.

The catkin looked over the edge at them in surprise, before speaking.

"Nyah! Sorry, I dyidn't see ya there! I'm Elsie! How cyan I help ya?"

"We heard we can claim the bounty on some bandits if we turned in their Thieves' Guild tokens here?" Diane said.

"Nyah? You're claiming the bounty on some bandits? Nyow how did ya myanage that? I byet these aren't even going to byee real tyokens. If it's a scyam, then scram!"

Thistleman passed the tokens up to the catkin, quieting the laughter of some of the adventurers behind them. Elsie looked at the tokens for moment, then back at Diane and Thistleman. Then she looked back at the tokens. She then pulled out a monocle from her green vest, and looked at the tokens through the monocle.

"These are indyeed legitimate tyokens," Elsie said, clearly dumbfounded.

"Then I would like my pay for them please." Diane was quite tired, but she still maintained her professional business sense.

Even if her family despised her, she'd still had a proper noble upbringing.

"Hymmm, nyormally we don't pay non-adventurers for quests, but syince these byounties were posted by the town guard, they asked us to pay anyone who cyollected on thyem. Syince the byandits hyadn't byeen myuch trouble, the reward is oynly forty silver cyoins and thirty-eight cyopper cyoins. Anything else I cyan help you wyith?"

"I would also like to register to become an adventurer with my servant, Thistleman."

Elsie's tail immediately stiffened. The other adventurers nearby became deathly silent, before erupting in laughter.

"First, this girl claims a bounty on bandits, and now this child wants to become an adventurer?!" A beady-eyed man grinned incredulously.

"Hahahaha, come back when you are old enough, kid!" A gruff man wearing a metal hat chortled.

Thistleman stared daggers into the crowd of adventurers.

These pathetic ingrates dare to laugh at her? She is my *master, and that alone puts her leagues above these worthless pissants!*

At the catkin's shocked silence, Diane continued, pointing at her crest and spoke with more determination. She was desperate, and after hearing the other adventurers' gossip about what they could earn and seeing what she just made, she knew she would have no better choice if she wanted to survive.

"I am Diane of House Culaine. I am pressing my right as a noble to register as an adventurer."

Some of the poorer noble houses would send their children to prove themselves as adventurers as a way to increase income, build status, and reduce their expenses on hiring people to train them. While it would normally be considered dirty for a great noble house to do the same, it was not entirely unprecedented.

Diane's declaration brought silence to the crowd, before an even greater round of laughter.

Thistleman was downright furious. His anger was overflowing into Diane, who barely managed to contain it herself.

"Well? I'm waiting." Diane puffed out her chest and placed her hands on her hips, staring with absolute determination into Elise's eyes.

The catkin sighed.

"Fine. Nyah. But when you regret it, dyon't come crying back to mye."

Chapter 8:
The Adventurer's Guild Exam

"This... this is just... highway robbery!" Diane exclaimed to Thistleman.

She was furious. The registration fee was an absolute outrage. Thirty-five silver coins. Thirty-five!

"Everything we just made, poof, gone! Just like that, and I might not even get an adventurer's card? And... AND! Another five silver to register you as my porter? I wish I asked Hal more about his time as an adventurer. If it seemed like I was going to get scammed, he would definitely have known what to do!"

Furious? Understatement. The way her whole body was shaking, you would think her blood was boiling.

" I WILL NOT ACCEPT THIS INJUSTICE! JUST YOU WAIT!!!"

My lips were sealed! Just nod and agree. It was all those damn assholes' fault that she was so angry. If only I was allowed to, I would have burned them alive, resurrected them, crucified them, and then burned them again for making me suffer through this indignity.

The doors to the examination room opened and a tall, slender man with brown hair, glasses, and a checkered vest entered the waiting room. He pushed his glasses back up his nose with his finger, before announcing, "Diane Culaine, you may enter now."

"About time! Thistleman, wait for me here. I will come get you when I get my guild card."

What was appropriate to say here? Surely it would be fine to go with an old daemonic line from back in the day.

"May you feast on the hearts of your enemies before their swords pierce you in the back!"

Perfectly delivered! And with a massive smile to boot!

The color drained from the proctor's face and Diane's back stiffened for a moment.

"Ahem, ah, right this way Diane."

The proctor looked between Diane and myself again. A strange feeling overcame him that today would certainly be an unusual day, and probably not in a good way.

The inside of the exam room was mostly empty except for three seats, two of which were occupied by a man and a woman. The man had a greying beard and bald head. A complete set of black full-plate armor with golden trimmings covering most of his body and a golden plate hung from a necklace. He projected a fierce attitude. The woman beside him was no less impressive, in spite of wearing only furs, as she held a massive battle-axe in one hand. She was clearly quite young, though her physique was impressive.

In the center of the room was a pedestal with eight small mana stones surrounding a blue rune tablet in the middle. Numerous circles, glyphs, and inscriptions covered the pedestal.

"Diane, please approach the pedestal. First, a small drop of your blood onto the tablet. Then, you will concentrate your mana on the array."

The proctor produced a small knife for Diane. She approached the pedestal, and enjoyed the shocked look of the proctor when she snatched the knife out of his hand without missing a beat.

"You want to see what I am made of? Well then, let us take a look!"

She flashed a grin as she made a larger-than-necessary cut across her hand, slightly suppressing a wince as she did so. Her blood dripped onto the rune and the inscriptions began to glow. She placed her hand on the side of the pedestal and started to focus her mana.

A mix of red and black auras began to fill the crystals, followed by an almost imperceptible flash of gold. Then, the glyphs began rearranging themselves with a fervor that enraptured her audience.

In the other room, Thistleman blinked. He had just felt something... strange.

Diane tapped her feet impatiently as the proctor stared at the rune plate.

"Well, what does it say? Do I have the potential or not?"

"Well... it appears like there is no issue with your potential," the armored man said.

"Certainly seems that way to me. So, which of us will observe the aptitude exam?" The woman asked.

"Neither of you, since I am the assigned proctor and you only came to observe. I've humored you this far because of your rank, but if you insist any further, I will kick you out. You do understand I can easily do that, right Sven? Right, Terra? I will not have you wreck the room again arguing over who will observe the test." As he turned away from them, the glint of a mythril plate shone out from under his vest.

"This is not fair, you always get the interesting ones!" Sven cried. "Come on Ye, at least let one of us watch!"

With surprising speed, he struck them both on the back of the head, knocking them unconscious.

"Alright Diane, this way to the aptitude exam. I have arranged for an iron plate adventurer to be your sparring opponent. I will be examining your abilities so feel free to go all out in this portion. I will intervene before you can get seriously hurt."

After they left the room, a pair of hooded individuals entered and removed the rune tablet, one glancing around furtively as much as the other strode assertively.

"Have you seen potential and abilities like these before?" The furtive man asked.

"Only for some of them, Eric." The other man replied simply.

"Are you sure she was a cripple?" Eric continued.

"I don't doubt our information network. She is indeed the daughter of the Culaine family. Plus, we watched the entire time. She clearly did not manipulate the exam."

"Some of this information… it is in a language I have not seen before. It feels ominous." Eric peered closely at the rune tablet, lifting his hood slightly to take a better look, the glow slightly illuminating his thin cheeks.

"It is probably an error. I have heard that can happen on very rare occasions." The other man assured him.

"Well, what should we do about it?"

"Clear it off. Only include relevant information for our records and the letter grade for her guild card."

"Her guild card? But she hasn't—"

"I am certain she will pass the exam. I look forward to watching it. Have Elsie prepare the welcome information as well. Our receptionists and attendants need to learn to have better attentiveness and insight for any of our current and potential members."

The man paused as he turned to leave. "And Eric, we will need to work quite a bit harder very soon here. The world you know…" He trailed off for a moment, then continued. "No, it's not of import yet."

Diane followed Ye as they entered the courtyard behind the guild hall. In the center was a large open pavilion with a wooden floor. Surrounding the pavilion were various small gardens and fountains, as well as training dummies and the staff quarters.

Numerous talismans had been hung around the pavilion.

"These talismans are for reinforcement and repair of the pavilion. Due to the nature of testing new adventurers, and the sometimes… explosive confrontations, we found it much more cost effective to invest in a fully enchanted pavilion rather than having it rebuilt every time."

"Oi, Ye, did you bring your kid here to watch the exam? Wasn't my opponent supposed to be with you instead?"

A tall, lanky man with short black hair, brown eyes, and a red bandana around his head yelled out to them. He was wearing decent chain armor with leather pants, fur boots, and he wielded a halberd.

A blood vessel throbbed slightly on Diane's forehead. "I'm right here! You... your attitude is terrible. You are definitely not worthy to face me!"

"Yup, she is right. You are definitely terrible."

"You tell him, Thistleman!" Diane did a double take. "Wait, what are you doing there?!"

Sitting on the branch of a tree with a particularly nice view of the pavilion, Thistleman grinned as he waved at them

"Me? Can't you tell? I am sitting."

Ye sighed before turning to the armored man. "Don't worry about it, Percival. He is signed up to become Diane's porter if she passes, so there is no need to worry if he watches."

"It's fine," Diane said. "He can sit there. But make sure you cheer your best for me, got it?"

"YOU GOT IT MISS DIANE! YOU'RE THE BEST! CRUSH HIM GOOD!" Thistleman started cheering and waving a small branch like a little flag.

Percival stood in the center of the pavilion, his eyebrow twitching violently.

Diane entered the pavilion and drew her rapier.

"You are to fight to your maximum ability," the proctor said. "The match will continue until I feel I have fully assessed your abilities, or if you are knocked unconscious. Ready? Begin!"

Diane felt a surge of energy filling her chest. She was feeling far more motivated now that Thistleman was watching. She launched herself at Percival, a fireball beginning to form in her left hand and a smile breaking out on her face.

Percival watched her come at him, noticing that her red aura was shot through with black. He jumped to the side as an orb of flames surging past him.

"What a foolish move, burning your trump card like tha—"

"*Fireball*!"

He rolled out of the way of a second fireball. What the hell was going on? All her energy should have been spent on the first fireball. Even after two, he could see that her mana wasn't diminished. But he didn't have time to think about what any of this meant as Diane was already upon him. Percival dodged and deflected the rapid strikes of her rapier. He swung low with his halberd to force her to jump back, giving him more room to unleash a combo.

"*Gravity Strike!*"

His blade hit the ground and a shockwave erupted. However, Diane dodged out of the way and sprinted up the shaft of his halberd.

"*Shit!*"

She lunged, her rapier aiming straight for his neck. Percival let go of his halberd and threw his right fist as hard as he could.

"*Goron Strike!*"

Red hot energy emanated from his fist as he aimed for Diane's belly. At least, that was what he planned before he and Diane were flung away from each other. In their midst stood Ye, wearing black gloves, his open palms facing each of them.

"That is enough. This fight is over. Diane, you qualify to become an adventurer. Please go see Elsie up in the front. Percival, come with me. Now."

"Woohoo! Go Diane! You did it! Way to qualify! You're the best!"

She couldn't wait for the day to be over, but she still had to finish up business here and they still had to find a place to stay. But at the very least, she figured she could close her eyes for a moment before finishing up business.

Chapter 9:
Welcome to the Guild!

GUILD CERTIFICATION CARD: DIANE CULAINE	Growth Potential: B	Aptitudes:
	Mana Capacity: 63	Magic (Fire) Melee (Rapier)
	Mana Regen: 3/??? Healing Factor: 1 Mana Reinforcement: 1.5 スピリチュアルアンプ	Skills: Fireball 悪魔の光景 共感リンク 悪魔の怒り
Contract Capacity Available: 0	Contracts Held: エラー	Power: 23
RANK: COPPER	Issuer: Njord A.G.	Exam Proctor: Mr. Ye Fan, Mythril Rank

All items marked in red are removed from Diane's Officially Issued Card. Contracts held marked as 0.

When Diane opened her eyes, she saw that she was lying on a couch with Thistleman curled up beside her. The catkin, Elsie, was leaning over them.

"What is going on?"

"Nyah, you're fyinally awayke. Gyood, I hyav some paperwork for you. I asked hyim, buy he syad he couldn't ryead."

Thistleman had been astonished to realize that despite his advanced age and his centuries of learning there were languages he couldn't read, and that he really was in an entirely different world. How was it that an all-powerful Demon Lord couldn't read? And so he remained in a fetal position, occasionally twitching as his mind kept trying to process his latest predicament.

"Ahahahahahahahaha. You two are certainly something special! You are an absolute riot! I haven't had a day this interesting in months!"

Terra's voice cut through Diane's tiredness while simultaneously being deeply annoying. Why the hell did she feel like the only adult in the room?

"Uuuwwuuuuu..." Diane moaned. "Finally, I'm finally done with all that paperwork."

Diane was sitting at a table in the main hall of the Adventurers Guild with Terra and a freshly recovered Thistleman. She looked exhausted and her face was covered with grime, caked in sweat and dried blood. Even the meal Terra had brought for them wasn't enough to perk up Diane.

"C'mon, forget the paperwork and eat up! You don't wanna stay so small and scrawny forever, do ya?"

Terra let loose with another thunderous laugh. Just as Diane was wondering why she was the only one seemingly having a good time, she received a smack on the back of her head from Terra's open hand. She went face-first into her meal.

"Ooooh, looks like you got your appetite back! Embrace your inner potato!"

Thistleman joined in with the laughter and Diane turned on him.

" YOU! WHAT MAKES YOU THINK I WILL LET YOU GET AWAY WITH THIS?"

Thistleman froze for a moment and Diane thrust her plateful of food into his face.

"Mmm, delicious, thanks!"

"That was my meal! Give it back!"

Terra completely lost her composure and fell back, knocking the table over in the process and laughing hysterically.

"OH! Oh, oh, that was good. Ah, so great. So, thanks for that. Tell ya what, let me make it up to you. In exchange for giving me such a good laugh, how about I teach you a thing or two about adventuring?"

Terra stood up and righted the table and seats.

"You're going to teach me about adventuring?" Diane said.

She perked up at the thought of tips from a veteran adventurer, particularly one with a gold rank, and forgot about her rapidly disappearing meal.

"First thing any adventurer needs is a decent map! Now, since y'all are new, I doubt you can find or afford one. But lucky for you, this gal here has an excellent memory!" Terra smiled as she pulled out a quill, an inkwell, and some paper. "Hmmm, I'm pretty sure this went here, and I heard about those reptiles from Sven… ah! I think Elsie forgot to tell you about the ranking system!"

"The ranking system?"

"Before the system was established, there was a huge problem with dangerous quests causing the loss of a lot of young and reckless adventurers. This caused manpower shortages around the world and made it hard to protect and manage the various realms. To mitigate this, the guild created the ranking system for parties and quests, in order to best match appropriate challenges to appropriate adventurers After proving themselves, adventurers earn the right to rank up.

"Now the advancement exam only applies to the lower end of guild ranks, which are Copper, Bronze, Iron, and Silver. Gold is the last rank that you have to take the exam in order to become Mythril. After that, the guild will promote you based upon enough achievements within that rank. Ya follow?"

Diane nodded her head.

"Now, your proctor today is probably the top Mythril rank in this guild hall. Now as for the higher ranks, we have Quicksilver, which is the minimum rank to apply to be a guild branch manager. Then, we have Orichalium and Adamantine. When the current guild master resigns, the next one is offered the position from the top of Adamantine on down to Orichalium. So far, only Adamantium adventurers have become guild masters, but Orichalium* is kept as an option because at this point there are so few Adamantium adventurers that if they all refused, we would be in quite the pickle! Lastly, we have Dragonscale, and these are absolutely legendary adventurers who almost everyone knows about. First we have a team we call the Three Samurai. They are made up of an oni, a youkai, and an akuma, and nobody has ever even seen their faces! Then we have the Walking Fortress Blanc, he is a dragonkin who only ever works alone. The last Dragonscale in the guild is the Fire God Byron, he is the first human to make the rank and brought the rest of his five man party with him. Of the Dragonscales, he definitely boasts the greatest firepower, but the way he uses his team, and his attitude… he is just such an asshole!"

Innocently, Diane asked, "But Terra, why do you think he is such an asshole? Doesn't being a Dragonscale sound super cool and important?"

"You will learn this in the future, but men, they are terrible, horrible, swines! He dared to say I was too muscular and unrefined. My natural beauty?! My tempered bosom! My—"

Terra stopped as she realized her terrible mistake. Silence filled the hall as Diane started giggling and soon the hall erupted in laughter.

"Did you hear? Terra got rejected by Byron!"

"What? That woman was crazy enough to ask him out? No way!"

"Everyone knows Byron isn't in to her type!"

Terra's face turned a fascinating pink, and she stopped drawing the map.

"I… I… I have to go!"

Terra shoved the map towards Diane, who was now laughing full-heartedly. She looked at the poorly scribbled map and realized it was definitely missing a lot of important details.

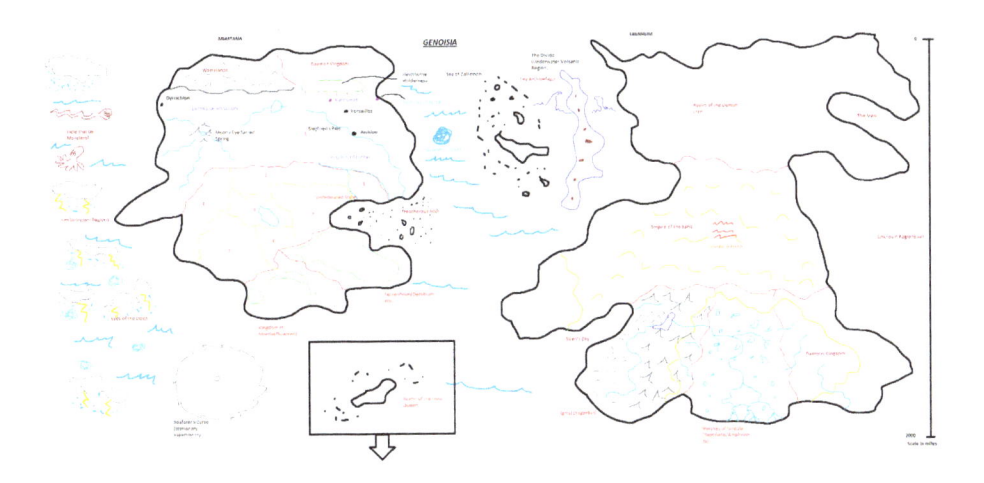

**Orichalium is for the rank, Orichalcum is the mineral. Which is not like Adamantium, which is used for both.

Chapter 10:
The Skeever and the Bear

The temperature was beginning to drop rapidly as the sun fell. Even in the late summer months, Njord was always extremely cold due to its northerly location and proximity to ocean. This was compounded by the constantly overcast sky. While residents were used to the climate and dressed appropriately, Diane was still wearing her same purple and gold hemmed dress she'd arrived in.

As she and Thistleman followed the winding road, the path began to narrow. There were a few stragglers coming in from hunting or fishing trips but before long, the streets were empty. As the last rays of sunlight disappeared and night fell, a freezing cold wind blew down the narrow alley. Some of the streetlamps began to illuminate in piecemeal fashion. Due to the poor economy of the neighborhood, the mana stones of some had not been replaced. Others flickered with a dying light as they reached the end of their supply.

Just as she was beginning to lose hope that they would find an appropriate and affordable inn, Diane saw a small sign hanging off one of the buildings. The sign read 'The Skeever and the Bear' and had a small picture of a bed next to it, indicating an inn. The building itself didn't look too run down, and unlike a few other establishments they had passed by, there were no shady characters standing outside. A warm yellow light poured out of its windows, which were protected by metal bars and the sound of laughter could be heard within.

"Thistleman! Here, this is where we are going to stay tonight."

"It definitely smells pretty good, so it should definitely be plenty safe!"

"Let's hurry inside and get out of this cold!"

Behind the bar stood a giant humanoid, over six feet tall. His arms, legs and chest were almost completely covered in brown fur, except for his face. His eyes were larger than a normal person's and were brown like his fur, while his front teeth were larger and sharper than a normal human's and they could see a pair of sharp top and bottom incisors when he opened his mouth for a big yawn. Behind him, right above his butt, a small brown puff ball of fur made up his tail, protruding over the top of his trousers. He wore a large plaid shirt. Behind him a massive woodcutting axe was mounted over the kitchen's fireplace.

He was holding a piece of cloth as he cleaned a large pewter mug. The barman was an ursine called Jotuun and was co-owner of the inn with the small woman who was busy ladling the remaining soup from a large cauldron into a container for storage. She was much shorter than Jotuun, standing at just under five feet tall. Her face was elongated, much like a large mouse, with a pink nose and black eyes. She was covered in grey fur but had on a pink dress and a white, stained apron. Behind her, a long tail poked out from a hole cut in to the back of her dress. She was a skeever who went by the name of Ryme.

About a third of the tables in the dining area were full with demi-humans and humans. There were even a couple of large orc laborers, each taking solitary tables. Two humans sat at the counter, each enjoying their ale and dinner. The walls were decorated with pictures and mounted monster heads, lit by mana lamps

Jotuun watched from behind the counter as a small, dirty girl, wearing a fancy yet fairly damaged purple dress, pushed the door open with the help of a small boy who was dressed in tattered peasant clothing. The girl seemed to stare in surprise at the demi-humans, and then himself.

"Jotuun, can you be a dear and greet the guests? I'm a little busy over here."

Ryme spoke sweetly and with a melodic tint. Jotuun nodded and lumbered up to the girl and boy as the door swung shut behind them.

"Welcome to the Bear and Skeever. Jotuun, Bear. Ryme, Skeever. Come sit. Leftovers only, but warm."

"Thank you, Jotuun, but I would like to pay for a room first." She passed Jotuun the pouch with her remaining forty-eight copper coins.

"How long can I get with this much?"

"One week. Dinner after sunset, breakfast at sunrise. Don't miss. Now come, sit."

Jotuun reached down behind Diane's head and grabbed the collar of her dress, effortlessly lifting her as he carried her to bar and the plopped her onto one of the stools.

"Thistleman, don't laugh at me! How come you didn't grab him too?"

"Could tell. He follow food. You prideful. Would say no."

Thistleman nodded. "Yep, yep, you hit it Uncle Bear!"

Diane turned as she heard chittering of laughter. The skeever smoothly slipped two bowls of steaming stew in front of the kids. Diane eyed the bowl ravenously.

"I'm Ryme, nice to meet you!"

"I'm Diane, and this here is Thistleman. He is my servant who I found in some bushes. Although saying his full name is a little long, so I kinda wanna give him a nickname."

"How about you call him Thistle—a nice, easy nickname that suits how thin he is!"

"Thistle, I like it!"

"Okay," Thistleman said grudgingly. "Thistle it is then"

He decided that enough was enough for one night. For the sake of his pride and sanity, he decided to just go to sleep. His head hit the counter, and he made damn sure to promptly start snoring.

"Oh, the little dearie passed out from exhaustion."

"Hm. Don't waste food. Diane, you eat. Then clean and rest. I'll take Thistle up now."

When Diane came in to the room after taking a quick bath, she saw Thistle had rolled himself off the bed and was sprawled, snoring, on the floor. Ignoring him, she curled up in the warm sheets and grabbed a pillow.

All the emotions she had been bottling up came bubbling to the surface. Hal, Sir Gregory, her father, the coachman, the bandits she had killed... She was scared. She was so very scared. She didn't know what to do next. Worst of all, she felt so alone, so very alone.

"I'm sorry. I'm so sorry, everyone," she kept repeating quietly to herself as she sobbed.

Then she heard Thistle rustle a little as he turned over in his sleep. She turned to look at him. No, she wasn't alone. Hal was wrong about at least one thing in his life, not all peasants will abandon you. She felt calm start spreading through her chest, allowing her to submit to her exhaustion and finally sleep.

As her eyes closed, Thistleman opened one eye to look at her. He had a strange expression, almost as if in pain or confusion. He silently mouthed the words "Sleep soundly" before he closed his eyes again. Outside the door, a small shadow quickly flitted in the direction of the dining room.

The hills outside of Njord were particularly windy and cold that night. A beautiful woman stumbled towards a door into the hillside, her left hand fumbling to open the latch. As the door opened, she was greeted by dim torchlight. The woman had three deep cuts across her midriff and blood was dripping from her face and shoulder-length black hair.

She closed the door behind her and stumbled to a nearby chest at the foot of one of the six beds in the cave. Amala pulled out a light red potion and poured it on her wounds. The bleeding stopped and she pulled out a large roll of bandages. She wrapped her wounds as best as she could manage before placing the bandages back in the chest.

Amala dropped onto a bed and covered her eyes with her left arm. Everything had gone so wrong. She had barely escaped from the dire wolf, and could still remember its razor sharp teeth shredding her arm and clamping onto the bone. She'd had to dislocate her arm so she could flee. In the process, the wolf's claws had ripped through her unprotected stomach. She ran as fast as she could back to the group, and the dire wolf started chasing after. She returned to the carriage only to find everyone dead and the horses gone. In a sense, she was thankful as the dire wolf had gone after their corpses—an easy meal.

Now, she wasn't sure what she was going to do. What good was an archer who could no longer use a bow?

Chapter 11:
My First Quest

As sun rose, small rays of its welcome, golden light began to poke through over the rooftops and the tips of the pine trees. Diane was greeted by the smell of cooking eggs and biscuits. She was so excited and full of energy, she hardly felt like the same girl from the night before. She practically ran over Thistle on her way out the door, grabbing her freshly cleaned dress and quickly throwing it on as she hurried towards the stairs.

"Thistle, wake up lazy bones! You don't want to miss breakfast!"

Thistleman stirred slowly, before yawning and sitting up. His need for food was a lot less than that of a person, and for some reason, the idea of taking the morning slow appealed to him. It was an odd feeling, not having to be worried about being murdered in your sleep. He had no grand ambitions. Yes indeed, he was a lazy bones! Though he didn't want to miss breakfast! There was a big smile on his face, which lasted for a grand total of three seconds.

Wait. Did I really just think that?

All the energy drained out of him as he realized the terrifying truth: he had escaped one horrible mind-altering influence, only to fall in to the hands of one even more overwhelming. She kept redefining who he was. He had severely underestimated the power of contracts. No wonder so few daemons offered them.

"Well, I suppose I better go get some breakfast too, but not because I don't want to miss it!"

Thistleman declared this to himself, unconvincingly trying to reassure himself he was not being influenced by her.

Ryme had heard Diane crying in her room the previous night and her heart had broken for the girl. Now, that same girl came flying down the stairs. She looked absolutely adorable now that she was all cleaned up!

"Good morning, little dearie! Hop onto the stool by the counter and I will have your breakfast right up!"

"Thanks, Auntie Ryme! It smells so great!"

"A-Auntie?!" she exclaimed, followed by a squeak. Ryme blushed a little.

"Yes, you are Auntie Ryme, and he is Uncle Jotuun!"

"If me Uncle, you Niece," Jotuun said, carrying in a tray. He patted Diane on the head with one of his massive paws and as she started giggling.

"Hey, you're messing up my hair, stooooooop!"

"Here you go," Ryme said, placing her breakfast before her. "I hope you enjoy it!"

Thistleman slowly walked down the stairs, taking a good look at the layout of the inn. Aside from Jotuun, there was little security and inn struck him as not particularly well defended. He would need to educate Diane, and hopefully the owners as well, on ways to improve this place with magical wards and dimensional expansion.

Thistleman groaned loudly as he climbed up onto his stood.

"Well aren't you the groggy looking one today, and here I thought with you getting more sleep than Diane!" Ryme hit Thistleman with a bright smile.

Thistleman started eating a biscuit extremely slowly with an empty, deadpan stare.

"Can we get a table for five? A double order of the breakfast special please. We got a request for some tivia wood from up in the mountain and got a long haul ahead. Can't waste these clear skies, and we will need the energy!"

"Coming right up! Jotuun, please get their table ready!"

As Thistle looked back down on his plate, he realized it was empty. He had been so focused on proving his mental independence to himself, he hadn't noticed that Diane has stolen the rest of his breakfast. Well, he wouldn't have stopped her from doing so anyway. The faster she healed up and grew, the faster he could recover himself too. He broke out into a big grin.

"Hehe, its fine. Deedee here has enough energy for the both of us."

"Who are you calling Deedee? Only I can give out nicknames! Its Diane, got it? Miss Di-ane! Anyways, thanks for the food, Auntie! We are running out to grab another quest from the guild. We will see ya tonight! Bye Uncle Jojo!"

Diane grabbed Thistle by the collar as she hopped off her stool, practically dragging him out the door. A few of the people of breakfast looked up and saw the expression of defeat on Thistleman's face.

She could hear Ryme call after them, "All right, be safe out there!" as well as a grunt of approval from Jotuun.

A minute later, the sound of a dropped plate smashing on the floor could be heard followed by a shocked squeak.

"Wait... did she say a quest?! JOTUUN, DID SHE SAY SHE WAS GOING ON A QUEST?"

The guild was bustling with activity this morning. Many lower rank adventurers were aiming to take advantage of the great weather to complete their quests. Elsie was worried this might be the last time she would see the guild this full of adventurers for a while. Only the higher ranked adventurers tended to have the budget to afford to travel. The implications meant that there would be fewer adventurers willing to take on the local quests, and that there would be inherently higher risk for the remaining adventurers, even if their groups barely met the mission qualifications.

Thankfully, the guild anticipated this mass migration of adventurers and kept a sizable emergency fund for situations like these. In order to compensate, the guild would post a gathering quest to purchase supplies of the ingredients for low tier healing potions. They even hired a full-time alchemist to produce potions for the guild, which they would sell at a slight loss to the adventuring parties, enabling them to reduce losses until the wars or subjugation missions ended, and the adventurers started coming back to their home branches.

Elsie bounced on her feet as she made her way to the quest board. "Nyah, listen up! Cyopper rank gyathering quest is now open! Please cyome to the cyounter to accept this quest!"

Catkin were almost always full of boundless energy, and even though she was apprehensive about the guild's current situation, and the higher-than-anticipated departures of adventurers (after all, dwarven-crafted gear is quite hard to come by), she had a very excited expression as she announced the quest.

Almost immediately, two groups showed up as takers.

The first was a group of two men, one woman, and one male canian. The canian was clearly the front line fighter, with decent leather armor, a small wooden shield, and an iron sword. Among the humans there was an archer, a rouge-like fellow with a short sword and daggers, and a female sorcerer wielding a much-too-large staff and an overly wide-brimmed hat. All of them wore copper plates on their chests and were fairly young, likely between nineteen to twenty years old.

"Good morning Elsie, we are here to pick up the gathering quest!"

"Nyah, its gyood to see you again, Randall! Hiya Jeanne, and Haraldr!"

"Hey Elsie!" Haraldr replied.

"Morning," Jeanne said.

Once Elsie got to the canian, they both started staring daggers at each other. Much like their distant ancestors, catkin and canians harbored a strong dislike of each other. However, she was the guild official. So instead, she chose to silently ignore Roofus.

"Here, I hyave the quest details for you."

Elsie proceeded to pass a small sheet over to Randall, which listed the items to collect along with pictures of them.

"Stay syafe out there. Good lyuck, nyah!"

"Thanks Elsie!" Randal replied.

As Elsie waved the group out the door, she heard a very loud, "Excuse me? What about us? We're here for the gathering quest too!" from below the counter. She looked over the edge again, and saw the small girl from yesterday standing there, tapping her feet impatiently.

"Hmmm, so according to this pamphlet, we need crow grass, tonba berries, and tuffle weed? Let's see… they are paying twenty copper per ounce collected."

Diane and Thistleman were walking out of the city. In their exhaustion the night before, they had left their horses at the guild, and by the time they had returned that morning, they were gone.

Thistleman looked over Diane's shoulder as she read aloud, trying to piece together the words on the page. At the very least, he could connect the words to the corresponding pictures.

"It seems the crow grass is not too hard to find, as it usually grows in sunny patches within the woods. It gets its name from the berries near its base, which tend to attract lots of crows to feed on them. However, the part we need is actually the stem, as the berries themselves are toxic to creatures other than birds.

"Next, we need the tonba berries, and the tonba berry bush grows on rocky areas on the side of mountains. So that one will also not be too hard. The tuffle weed will be harder to find, as it only grows near streams, is apparently rare, and tends to look like the other local plants. What we need from it is the flower, which only opens in the afternoon when the sun is out, and it has a very identifiable crimson color when it does. Luck-yyyy! I knew it, today is finally, really going to be my lucky day!"

Thistleman thought he had heard rumors long ago about something called a jinx, but he decided not to say anything about it as he didn't want to dampen her enthusiasm.

Randall, Haraldr, Jeanne, and Roofus were very excited. Today had gone exceedingly well. They had managed to get a decent supply of crow grass and tuffle weed. All that was left were the tonba berries, which they saved for last as it was the farthest away, and easiest to find on the mostly barren mountainsides. They had already gathered quite a few, but wanted to evenly match their supply of crow grass and tuffle weed to maximize their reward.

"With this much, we should at least be set for the next month! Maybe we can finally get me a new spell book too??" Jeanne was excited. Learning new spells was an extremely difficult and expensive task for individuals who were not part of a major noble family.

"I might get me a new bow!" Randall said.

"Heh, enjoy your gear. I think I want to use my share for some... more discreet pursuits." Haraldr had a somewhat perverted look on his face. He had seen the ladies at some of the brothels in the slums, and had always dreamed of losing his V-card. However, due to his shady personality, he could never win any girls the normal way. For him, the brothel was a godsend. Plus, he'd just turned twenty and was officially old enough to enter.

"Ugh, you're so gross, Haraldr. This is why you can never pick up any girls."

"Yeah, well why would I need to worry about picking up girls when I can just pay for them?"

"Because regular girls are much better and cleaner! You don't know what the girls, or guys, in a brothel have!"

The two quickly halted their fight when Randall raised his fist, halting the group. Roofus was scouting ahead, using his keen wolf senses to look for monsters. They could hear him howling in agony.

"Hurry, up around the cliff face!"

Randall dropped his pack with their supplies and drew his sword, Haraldr readied a pair of daggers and stepped back into the tree line, and Jeanne brought up the rear. When they got close to the corner of the cliff, they could hear a loud buzzing noise. Randall held in his breath. He could smell the strong scent of blood, and he could hear the chittering and popping of insects, as well as a mushy, crunching noise.

Randall held his breath, closed his eyes for a moment, before opening them again and looking around the corner.

He saw Roofus, or what was left of Roofus, being shredded by a swarm of giant, red-eyed hornets. Each one was at least the size of a small boulder, measuring about six feet in length and three feet tall. Their mandibles made quick work of his flesh, and crunched through his bone and armor effortlessly.

Roofus's disembodied hand was holding on to the small stem of a tonba berry bush. In his excitement, it seemed he hadn't noticed the holes dotting this side of the cliff, marking the giant hornet nest.

Randall couldn't hold in a gasp at the sight, and immediately threw up. The noise caught the attention of the hornets and the swarm started flying.

"RUN!" Randall screeched as loudly as he possibly could.

However, as he began to run, he felt the ground start to slip away from under him and a strong pressure grabbed his waist. Then, an extremely sharp pain cut through his shoulder. He was screaming in agony as he looked over and saw the giant mandibles, easily slicing through his flesh. That's when he felt the pain shoot through his leg, as another hornet came from underneath and latched on.

Haraldr stood in the trees, watching in horror as he saw Randall's body stretch and then rip, his blood and organs raining down. Jeanne was pinned beneath a swarm on the ground, her screams quickly turning into gurgles, and then all that was left were the sounds of chittering, crunching bones, and tearing meat.

He regained his senses and tried to quickly move away from the gruesome scene, stifling his urge to retch and hoping he hadn't been noticed.

Please, god, if you're out there, don't let them have noticed me!

Chapter 12:
Of Horror and Hornets

A chorus of howls reverberated through the forest as Diane ran with Thistleman towards the mountain. Today had gone far more poorly than Diane could have anticipated; her hopes from earlier in the morning had been dashed.

At first, things hadn't been too bad. They had found a few patches of crow grass by following the birds flocking in the sky. Shortly afterwards, they stumbled across a stream. and while it had mostly been picked clean of tuffle weed, they were soon able to find a few patches. However, things turned south as soon as Thistle seemed to catch wind of something. He said it smelled like a pack of dire wolves and they were heading in their direction. They quickly moved towards the mountain, trying to get lost amongst a herd of thunder deer, which locals sometimes called styars. They were strange creatures that could shoot lightning from their horns, but were mainly peaceful.

As soon as it saw them, the herd made a sharp turn, leaping over them and then cutting away across the river. And now, the dire wolf pack was on their trail. Mistakenly, Diane wondered how the day could get any worse.

Haraldr was dashing through the woods as fast as his legs could carry him. He was terrified. Behind him, he heard the buzzing of two, maybe three giant hornets.

"HELP! SOMEONE, ANYONE, HELP!"

He dodged two hornets coming from both sides only for a third to drop out of the sky above him.

At that moment, he heard a loud chorus of howls. Dire wolves. The gods had abandoned him. He couldn't help but laugh. The only thing worse than giant hornets were dire wolves. Even as the giant hornet's mandibles tore into him, he couldn't stop laughing. He didn't even notice the two kids running towards him. One of them yelled something and the girl leaped onto the hornet. It took off, still holding him in its claws and he never stopped laughing.

"Diane, jump on the hornet now! Use your rapier to stab into its back and hold on!"

"What? Are you crazy? That thing is huge and disgusting!"

"So what? It's better than the direwolves! Don't worry, I have a plan! We will use the hornets to get out of here!"

Diane looked at the massive bug with absolute disgust. The other two hornets had fled back to the mountain at the sound of the dire wolves' approach. This last one was too distracted with its prey to notice the incoming threat.

As the chorus of howls rose in volume behind her, she sprinted and leapt onto the giant hornet's back, stabbing down with her rapier. The point of the blade hits its carapace and bent, denting the chitin but otherwise failing to pierce it.

"Shit I need more power!"

She closed her eyes as the hornet rose in the air. She focused her mana into her rapier and stabbed again. The blade pierced the chitin and lodged into the muscle beneath, helping her to hang on.

"Thistle! Thistleeee!!!!"

"Don't worry about me, I'll be fine! Just no matter what, hold on!"

The pack of dire wolves erupted from the brush and Thistleman promptly disappeared back into the foliage, heading towards the mountain.

Tears start filling her eyes and Diane was gripped by an indescribable anger. She was angry at everything, but most of all, she was angry at herself for being so weak. She could feel the surge of rage filling her, energizing her. Her muscles began to tremble in anticipation. She just wanted to destroy them all.

Thistleman cursed to himself as he ran from the dire wolves, leading them to the mountain.

"*Devils Sight!*"

His eyes focused on the hornet carrying Diane. He could also see a young man, oozing blood and laughing to himself. At the very least, he was thankful for that idiot giving Diane a way out of this mess. He was having incredible difficulty coming up with a way to not only lose the dire wolves, but to do so in a way which didn't harm anyone or anything. He didn't want to experience the more severe consequences of violating the core tenets of his contract. Just breaking a small order hurt more than enough, and he was still so far from the zenith of his power.

Thistleman leaped over a large fallen tree, not too worried about keeping up appearances since he was out of sight of Diane. He looked back, and could see the drool flying out of the dire wolves as they chased him down.

Thistleman shook his head and continued his pursuit.

Diane could see the cliff coming in to sharp relief as the giant hornet approached it. Two other hornets flew in low for a moment, a strange powder dusting off their wings. As soon as they got close enough, she would finish off this hornet and get back onto solid ground, killing any others that got in her way.

Before she could execute her plan, a massive swarm lifted off from the ground, covered in blood from a recent feeding frenzy. More began to erupt from the cliff. The powder she had seen carried a warning pheromone that the hive was under threat.

However, the fury was already taking hold of Diane. A minute earlier, and she would have been lost in fear... but now, her plan was just to kill. She held on tight to her rapier as the wind started to pick, causing her hair to unravel and flow behind her. A black and red aura began to cloak her body.

She grabbed onto a wing joint and pulled her blade out of the hornet's back, before stabbing it in the eye, piercing its skull and brain. The giant hornet began to descend rapidly. However, Diane didn't want to land... not yet. A the swarm began to thicken and fly towards her, she leaped off the back of the hornet, stabbing straight into the mouth of another hornet. The blood started to rain down.

She started to smile, a mad laugh escaping her lips. Another hornet was coming up from below. Perfect, it would help her ride higher into the skies!

Thistleman saw the massive swarm rising in the distance. This was bad, really bad. Even with the dire wolves as a distraction, there were far too many hornets. No matter how much mana he provided to Diane, eventually they would swarm over her, and she would be torn to pieces. The dire wolves would have no problems killing large numbers of hornets, but they would be nowhere near fast enough.

Shit! What do I do?

As he brought the dire wolf pack close to the hornet's nest, he could see Diane leaping between hornets in the sky, dropping them like flies. The smell of fresh blood excited the pack into a frenzy.

"*Warp.*"

Thistleman disappeared from in front of him, but the dire wolves didn't worry about it for a moment. Now they had new prey. One of the wolves sprinted up the side of a large tree, leaping off of it and snatching a hornet out of the air. The wolf was easily twice its size, and the hornet came crashing to the ground. With a single, precise bite, the dire wolf tore the head off the hornet. Immediately, the other dire wolves started to do the same, methodically ripping giant hornets from the air and beheading them. Swarms of hornets began to descend in a desperate defense against the wolves. Giant hornet larvae were a delicacy to the dire wolves, and if they made it into the nest, without a doubt all the larvae would get eaten, the queen would be killed, and the hive would die off.

These were not, however, Thistleman's concerns. He needed to help Diane.

An extraordinarily sharp pain cut through his shoulder. His eyes, wide, Thistleman looked but couldn't see a wound.

"What the...?"

He doubled over, the pain much worse. Diane saw him and, distracted, the claws from one of the hornets cut through her shoulder. He couldn't imagine what he would suffer if she died, but that pain... he'd never felt anything like it before. An absolute, piercing, unstoppable pain. The consequences of breaking his contract scared him.

Then... he had a realization. He could still help Diane without killing, and he could also do so without any "demonplay", as she had once put it. He simply could be both—a demon and her little peasant. But... he also wanted her dead. He wanted out. Or did he? Fulfilling the contract meant he would keep his life, but then, did that mean that failing it would....?

"AHHHHH, DAMN IT ALL! Here we go!" He'd made his decision. Her will, her authority, he would accept it as absolute.

Diane Culaine, Master of Demons, don't let me down!

"*Hall of Mirrors*, I call upon you, and cast my vision in perfect clarity. *Mirror Image*! *Warp*! By the art of the skies, unbounded by law, I defy you! *Levitation!*"

A perfect copy of Thistleman appeared before him, before he disappeared high into the sky above the mountain. Now for the finale. There was one trait all creatures shared and that was fear. If this failed then nothing would work. He would release his aura and, with it, a cloud of powerful miasma. He had never seen a creature that didn't flee from his approach when his powers were unleashed.

"From the farthest pits of hell, I call upon the powers of shadow and darkness! Show my true form and unleash despair!"

His body quickly morphed, its height rapidly increasing and mass returning to his formerly scrawny limbs as a massive fog of miasma began to explode from his body. The Demon Lord of Destruction was making an appearance.

The pain in her shoulder was intense but Diane couldn't let up now. She couldn't die. Thistle was waiting for her down below.

She managed the leap on top of another hornet, stabbing it through the head. She was afraid, and was losing blood quickly. She couldn't keep this up. She felt a burning sensation in her chest. It was something she had never experienced before and caused her to double over in pain, holding tightly onto the giant hornet's falling corpse.

On her chest, the mark began to glow and spread. She had been accepted as the master of a contract, her new status seared into her flesh. From the seal, she could feel an overwhelming power and a sea of emotion. She looked up to see a huge, dark cloud, growing and spinning faster and faster. An aura, dark and terrible, rained down on the creatures below. The hornets, the direwolves, even the bugs and birds, all of them were fleeing.

"PITIFUL CREATURES! WHO DARES TO STAND IN THE PRESENCE OF ONE WHO I HAVE ACKNOWLEDGED AS WORTHY OF BEING MY MASTER? BEGONE, OR FACE THINE END!"

The air and earth shook at the proclamation and large boulders came loose, tumbling down the mountain. The authority of the first and eldest Demon Lord, even in his weakened state, was not something any ordinary creature could look down upon or face.

Diane's vision was becoming blurry, and she could barely see the outline of the being at the center of the maelstrom. She couldn't hold on anymore and passed out.

Diane woke up a short while later. Night had fallen and she was next to a small fire. Her shoulder had some fresh bandages around it, and Haraldr was lying nearby, also patched up. Thistleman worked fervently at the pot over the fire.

She was about to sit up and speak, when Thistleman held up a finger to shush her.

"Save your energy. You're really hurt."

Both of them were gravely injured and wouldn't survive a rough journey back into town. However, Thistleman was in the process of attempting to make a healing brew.

The moment he saw the first bubble rise, he pulled the pot off the heat. Then, he took out the tonba berry paste he had made and mixed it with the brew. He breathed a sigh of relief it turned a light pink color.

"Alright, Diane, relax. It's going to be a little warm."

"Ok. I trust you."

She winced a little when the brew was poured on her shoulder, but then started to relax as the pain faded.

"That... feels a lot better. Since when did you learn to make potions?"

"I... I saw someone doing it when I was young. I was just trying to improvise from what I saw."

That wasn't a lie. He had seen someone working on potions when he was young. Over ten thousand years ago.

"Ok, seems I have a bit left over. Not the strongest stuff, but it will save his life."

He walked over and poured the potion on Haraldr's numerous wounds. Some of them started to close over a little, and a very thin membrane of skin covered the larger gashes. His labored breathing stabilized.

"Alright, he should be fine to be moved now. Diane, can you walk?"

"Y-yes, I should be fine!"

She carefully stood up and made sure not to move her damaged shoulder too much. In the darkness, they carefully and quietly made their way back into town.

Chapter 13
Prize and a Party

Tonight, the guild hall was quieter than usual. There were a couple of groups of adventurers sitting around some tables, making plans for the following day, but the vast majority of adventurers had packed up and left for the mercenary quests, with only the stragglers who couldn't get on any of the caravans or ships remaining in town.

Mr. Franz Falkiore was running the front desk tonight. He was a man of average height and a particularly slender build, known mostly for his... eccentricities. He wore white face paint, with a pair of small red triangles under each of his eyes. He also liked to wear funny-looking, frilly clothes and oversized red shoes. As to why he looked like that, he always said it was an old habit from a job in his previous life. Most people just took it as a joke, and treated it as another one of his eccentricities, along with his talk of magicless self-driving carriages and handheld communication blocks.

Since he had so much free time at the moment, he was working on another one of his odd pet projects. He was trying to create an odd, stretchy substance with which to make animal shapes after filling it with air. However, despite claiming it was a real thing, he had never learned the appropriate skills or knowledge to make it, since, according to him, he was "a high school dropout." Not that anyone had ever heard of one of those schools either. This never stopped him though; he relished his role as the madman.

He was so focused on his work, he didn't notice the main doors open, nor did he notice the kids walking up to the desk until they were just a few feet away. Seeing Diane covered in blood and guts, his immediate reaction was a little... extreme.

"Hmm, so if we try and adjust the formation here, and here, maybe I can repli—AHHHHH! IT'S A GHOUL, A ZOMBIE, A CREATURE BACK FROM THE DEAD! DON'T EAT ME, BABY ZOMBIE, I AM ONLY A CLOWN AND MY BRAINS DON'T TASTE THAT GOOD! Wait... ah? You aren't a zombie here to eat my brains? OH MY GOODNESS, you are a true to life real child! Well, I'll be, that is quite the amount of blood on ya! Gave this ossan a good old heart attack, you did! Now how can good old Mr. Franz help you?"

He pulled a tiny horn out of one of his pocket and blew into it twice.

Diane, who was covered in two types of blood and chunks of flying insects, was temporarily frozen in a look of shock, revulsion and... fascination at this strange display.

Thistle responded with a quizzical head-tilt. "You are a strange one, aren't you? So... what kind of monster person are you supposed to be? I have never seen this... clown-type humanoid before."

"What? *Me?* A--m-m-monster person? What could you possibly be getting at, good sir? Why, I bid you a good day!"

"It's night."

"Oh, so it is. You are quite right. Oh well! So then, corpse disposal fee is ten silvers, burial is another five, and... three gold in bribes to the city guard."

"This guy isn't dead."

"Oh, he isn't? A shame. You sure? He could be, for an additional ten silver."

"You... you aren't serious, are you? Because I can't afford that."

"The moon is quite pretty tonight, huh? I wonder, I heard it was made of cheese."

Diane definitely wasn't in the mood to handle this exchange. "This kid isn't dead. He is part of another adventuring group. The rest... didn't make it. Can you please take care of him? And not in the killing way? Also, Thistle, turn in the rest of the goods. I just want to get this over with and go back to the inn"

"Right away. Here you go!"

Thistle unceremoniously tossed Haraldr at Mr. Franz, glad he wasn't their problem anymore. Mr. Franz looked a little shocked, not only at having an injured, unconscious man literally thrown onto him, but at the ease with which the small boy did it. Then, he also noticed the overstuffed packs the boy was carrying. Something... was definitely off.

Then, the dump. A half-dozen giant hornet cores, thirty ounces of crow grass, thirty ounces of tuffle weed, and twenty-five ounces of tonba berries.

Mr. Franz looked carefully at the monster cores, before looking at the kids' plates.

"Where... did you get these?"

So Diane told him their story, although she conveniently left out the part about the demon she'd seen. She could hardly believe what had happened herself, so instead she focused on the slaughter of the hornets, making it sound more like the nest was cleared between her and the dire wolves.

She also said to give half the money from their reward to the unconscious Haraldr, since he would need it more than them. All in all, they had made one gold, twenty-eight silver, and fifty coppers from the quest.

Mr. Franz made a mental note to verify as much of the story as he could with Haraldr when he woke up. If true, he would need to have a very serious discussion with the branch manager or the assistant manager.

Back at the inn, Ryme was pacing back and forth with two plates of food long since cold.

Jotuun, on the other hand, was sitting down at one of the empty tables, his eyes locked on the door.

"Jotuun, its getting late. It is getting really late. They should have been back by now, right?"

"Mmm."

"They really did say they were going on a quest, right? But kids can't take quests. But if they did, they should have been back by now. So why aren't they back yet?"

"Mmm."

"You don't think they got hurt, do you? If they did, what should we do? Do you think the guard will look for them?"

"Mmm."

"They wouldn't listen to us anyways. They should have been here by now. I even made all this food for them. You don't think they aren't coming back, do you?"

"Mmm."

"They have to come back. They paid for a week, you agreed to a week right? Who pays for a week and then doesn't come back? Its rude! I will have to scold them for being rude guests!"

"Mmm?"

Jotuun's ears perked up and he rose from the table so quickly that Ryme squeaked and jumped in surprise. Jotuun rushed to the door when he saw the handle start to turn, grabbing the door and flinging it open.

Diane, surprised, fell through the entrance.

"Eeeeeeeeeiiiiiii!!!! I knew it. You really did take on a quest, didn't you? Reckless! Reckless little girl! And look at you, you're all hurt and covered in blood!"

Before she knew it, Diane was pounced on by the small skeever who immediately started fussing all over her.

"Jotuun, heat up their food! You, Missy, need to get cleaned up first! You are such a mess, ugh, and I just washed your dress last night! You need to stop treating such a nice piece of clothing so roughly. Reckless! You're reckless! And you… what are you carrying in that bag?"

Ryme finally noticed Thistleman standing near the door, clearly enjoying the show.

"Oh, this? It is our quest reward."

"Yeah, we got it for killing some giant hornets and gathering some stuff. Hey, Auntie! I have a new job for you! Since you're taking care of us, can you also handle the money too? I don't have anywhere else to keep it, and a good auntie would definitely help us out with it, right?"

Rhyme looked into the bag and squeaked again when she saw the large sum of money in there. They would take months to earn a gold coin here, especially after taking out living expenses from their daily earnings. Her entire body stiffened and the shock and stress caused her to faint.

Jotuun let out a loud, hearty laugh as he secures the door for the night.

"Niece and nephew do good! Finally, Ryme stop worry so much!" He reached down and picked her up, before setting her gently into one of the chairs around a well cleaned table.

"Hurry, get cleaned before Ryme wakes and gets mad. I heat up big, good meal!"

At the sound of all the noise downstairs, some of the other patrons come down the stairs.

"Hey hey, what's going on down here? It's getting a little noisy!" an elf chimed in.

"Niece and nephew finished first quest! We having party! They tell story after bath!"

"A party! Count us in. Woof!" A floppy-eared canian leading a small pack of his friends descended the stairs

"Hum? Did I hear you say your niece and nephew finished a quest? I would like to hear what kind of feat the family of the Mighty Jotuun accomplished! Let's get us a strong ale to go with it!" Even the solitary orcs had come down to join them.

"Aye Aye!" the rest of the patrons chanted in unison, and soon the dining hall was very lively indeed.

As Diane came down the stairs after her bath, she was shocked to be received by such a large, warm group. She did her best to tell the story again, with everyone listening attentively. It fulfilled their desire for a sense of adventure to hear the story coming from such a young girl. It also filled them with a sense of awe and pride, as she was able to accomplish things that even they could not.

Diane and Thistleman did not get to sleep until very late that night.

Mr. Franz was desperately trying to hunt down the branch manager. Shortly after the kids left, Haraldr woke up. He confirmed Diane's story. But it should have been impossible! An ten year old child, escaping from dire wolves and luring them into a giant hornet nest, slaughtering them, and getting away after? Such a thing had never been heard of before! The youngest noble to clear a giant hornet nest had been sixteen years old at the time, and he had a healer with him!

Mr. Franz had checked everywhere. Neither the branch manager nor the assistant manager were in their rooms, the lounge, the training area, or the pavilion, nor in any of the various offices off the hall. Finally, Franz found them on the highest patio in the building, looking out to the wilderness in the north.

"Ah, Mr. Franz, I was wondering when you would show up."

"S-sir, were you waiting for me?"

"Hmmm? Yes, I believe you have a report for me."

"How did you...?"

"It is of no concern. Please, continue."

"Well, it is about Diane. I have confirmation that she may well have cleared an entire giant hornet nest, and also lured dire wolves into helping her do so, and subsequently escaped from them."

"Hmmm, yes, and there is there something else you would like to ask?"

The branch manager's apparent disinterest was really throwing Franz off.

"Well, I believe proper procedure would be to send someone to verify the report, no?"

"There is no need for that. Actually, that area has become exceedingly dangerous since she left. Diane is quite the lucky girl. Raise the threat category of Brownrock Mountain to Orichalium. Post it as a guild announcement. Ah, and about Diane, we will submit the final report to the guild file. There is no need for you to worry anymore about this."

"Yes, you're right. There is no more need for me to worry any more about this. Thank you for your time."

Mr. Franz felt calm wash over him and he lost interest in pursuing the matter any further. He decided it would be best to continue to treat Diane and Thistleman as perfectly normal guild members.

"Was that the right thing to do?" The hooded assistant manager asked the branch manager after Franz had left.

"Undoubtedly. If she were to make such a huge wave upon first arriving here, it would bring the wrong kind of attention to Njord, don't you agree?"

"Well, it is possible. Particularly in the higher ranked adventurers. They may try and seize an opportunity to claim Diane for themselves or their teams. But would that be wrong?"

"I believe that girl deserves some privacy, don't you? We wouldn't want her to be snatched away from our guild, now would we? You do want to make it to branch manager, right?"

"Well, true. Do you think she is the key to do it? I mean, I never expected you to make branch manager before me, but I am still too far from being qualified. Also, why did you place a restriction on Brownrock Mountain?"

"I always fulfill my end of the deal. As for Brownrock... well, let's just say my intuition tells me something really nasty is moving in there. Ah, one last thing, since it would be too strange for us to do nothing here, we should upgrade Diane with the Special tag. It is usually given to individuals with notable potential, although lets avoid making a public declaration. We will also wait until she reaches an... appropriate age before allowing her to rank up."

"I suppose you are right, as usual."

The two hooded figures turned and went back into the guild. A powerful gust of wind snuffed out the torch as they walked through the doors into the guild hall.

Chapter 14:
A New Normal

The cold night wind howled outside the window, causing it to vibrate loudly. Diane had been having some difficulty going to sleep, her mind alight with questions and all kinds of thoughts.

Just *how* had everything worked out so well? She rolled over in the bed and opened one eye to look at Thistleman, sprawled out on the floor again.

"Hey, Thistle. You awake?"

"Always. Whatsup?"

"Well, I.... uh... about today. Did any of it... seem weird to you?"

"Hmmm, well that Haraldr guy sure seemed pretty happy getting all torn up. And the counter guy thought the moon was made of cheese. Why do you ask?"

"Well... I just... I thought you shouldn't think anything was weird and just get back to sleep. You're keeping me up!"

Diane turned back over in a huff. She realized she didn't have the confidence to ask what she really wanted to know.

Meanwhile, Thistleman opened his eyes and looked at her in confusion. Thus, the night passed, with Diane finally catching a few hours of sleep after getting over her embarrassment.

Diane jumped up with a start. The dim light of the day was peeking through her window,.

"How late is it? Thistle! Thistle! Get up! I think we missed breakfast! This is all your fault for keeping me up! What will I do if we don't get breakfast? What will I eat? Can I go on another quest while hungry? You better have a good answer for me!"

"Well, how do you know we missed breakfast?"

"Because I can't smell it! Plus, look how late it is! Ryme said that breakfast is at sunrise and it is well past sunrise!"

"You know, they kept a plate of dinner for us last night. Maybe they kept a plate of breakfast this morning too."

"But... what if they didn't?"

Thistleman was getting a little flustered. He had no idea how to handle this situation. Hunger was rarely a problem for daemons, and even then, only the weakest suffered from it

"Well, the only way to find out is to go down and check!"

"Then what do I do if they have nothing?"

"Well... I don't know, eat some moss or something! There is a lot of the growing around here!"

"YOU IDIOT!"

She struck him upside the head and Thistleman found himself almost regretting stopping her from getting eaten. Almost.

The morning had been a particularly busy one. Word was getting around from the other patrons about Diane's story, and that Jotuun had a niece and nephew in town. A lot of the locals were curious and wanted to meet them, and so Ryme found herself cooking nonstop almost all morning, and Jotuun had a lot of cleanup to do around the tables. Before she ran out of food, Ryme managed to stash a plate for the kids.

"I hear things are getting really heated amongst the nobles. Did you know Duke Vermillion and Count Horatio are preparing to go to war against each other?"

"What? How did that happen??"

"I heard he assassinated the count's son."

"That's outrageous! Why would he do something like that?"

"I dunno, noble minds are just different, I guess?"

"Woof, is that so? I heard he was aiming to kill his daughter and missed!"

"Nyah, his daughter? I heard it was her lover!"

"Hah! Neither of you are right! It is certainly the duke projecting a man's strength! Killing the count's son is a truly bold and time-honored way to declare war!"

"Time-honored for who? We aren't orcs. That's not how things work here!"

"Kyahahahaha! Then wrestle me, the winner will be who is right!"

"That doesn't matter, from what I heard it is even worse than that! My cousin is a squire to a knight back in the capital. Apparently, the king's brothers are using this fight to push their children's claim on the inheritance."

"What? How could the king allow this! What about his children?"

"Do you live under a rock? This is only a problem in the first place because *he has no kids*."

"Well, I for one have no interest in feuds. Njord has always followed the rightful king of Luthas. If there is no heir, when the king dies we will have no liege."

"Shhhh, you shouldn't say things like that!"

"Why not speak his mind? We are among brothers here!"

"WOOOOAH! The canian and orc are going at it! Who will win the arm wrestling contest?"

The bustling activity kept Ryme from hearing Diane's tirade to Thistleman. However, when she saw Diane appear at the top of stairs, she waved energetically and called out "Dearie, I saved you a plate!"

She wasn't sure if she had said something wrong but but Diane stopped in her tracks, her face turning bright red. Then she saw a despondent boy walk down next to her. When he looked her in the eye, she just got even redder.

What is wrong with kids these days? I just saved some breakfast for them.

Elsie was having a very odd day so far. First, when she came in this morning, Mr. Franz was behaving stranger than usual, and seemed out of sorts. She couldn't quite pin down what was wrong, and he didn't elaborate much other than shoving a small pile of papers into her furry mitts before wandering out the door, whistling to himself.

Then, as she sorted through the stack of papers, not only did she see that most of Randall's crew had died yesterday, which was an absolute disaster, but that Diane had managed to save their last member, completed the gathering quest, and killed some nasty monsters. What the heck was up with this report? Was Mr. Franz finally losing all his marbles?

Then... one of the guilds office assistants came in and delivered her the weirdest note yet.

"Here you go Elsie, an internal announcement straight from the top. For guild staff only."

"Nyah? What kynd of thing would..."

The soulless office drone had already turned around and started making his way back to his cubicle.

With a sigh, she closed an eye and glanced down at the bulletin. *What kind of crazy announceme*—both her eyes opened wide.

Diane Culaine has been promoted, with the official rank of Copper! She was hereby allowed to take quests, ignoring the usual rank restrictions, effective immediately. Elsie was hereby instructed to convey the guild's sincerest congratulations to Miss Diane at her soonest convenience, and to ensure all appropriate protocols were followed to prevent the excessive spread of this information, for Diane's privacy and convenience. Naturally.

Our sincerest congratulations on your new role, Elsie!

Assistant Manager: Eric von Straught

Branch Manager: Baal

Before she even had time to finish processing this information, the guild door was flung open. Huffing in the entrance was a small girl wearing a purple and gold hemmed dress, starting to fill with patches and stitches, most impatient at the late start to her day.

"ELSIE! I'm here for a new quest!"

Behind her, that peasant porter of hers smiled and waved.

"Nyah?!?!"

The cloud of miasma that was hanging around Brownrock Mountain was slowly condensing. In the thickest part of the cloud, a hand began to form, before reaching out and grabbing onto a nearby boulder. A shadowy body was slowly starting to materialize.

Who am I? What is my purpose? Why do I feel so... lost? Aimless?

Chapter 15:
An Unlikely Friendship?

"Nii-san, are you going out again?"

I saw the little girl again, a little older now, probably no older than Diane. Her bright blue eyes stared into mine. Her blonde hair had started to darken a little into a cute dirty blond.

"Just one more time. After this time, I won't ever have to leave you behind again. We will be able to stay in a nice little house and I can get you that doll you always wanted."

I spoke, but the words were not mine. I wanted out, but this kept happening to me, again and again.

"I hate it when you leave, because every time you go out, you always look so sad and hurt when you come back! I'm scared... I'm scared that one day you might not come back."

Stop it! stop stop stop!

"I do what I have to do. No matter what, I will always take care of you, Nina. Just wait for me here. I will be back, I promise!"

Thistleman sat up, fast as a bolt of lightning. His breathing was heavy. He wasn't even trying to sleep, yet every night for the past three weeks, he kept having these dreams. They were maddening. Who was this kid? She seemed familiar. She looked like the girl from the broach.

I need to find this kid. She has to know something.

Thistleman looked over at Diane, making sure she was sleeping soundly. She had charged in to the guild every morning since they'd arrived back from the mountain and had taken on a new quest every day. She wouldn't be waking any time soon.

Without even a hint of a sound, his body slowly melded with the shadows and slipped through the cracks in the ceiling.

It had been several weeks since Gus last left for his job and never came back. By the end of the first week, Nina had run out of food but she waited patiently in their little apartment. During the second week, she got so hungry she started begging for food. Most people ignored her, but she didn't know what else to do. She couldn't even imagine stealing from others, and so she just continued to suffer.

By the end of the second week, the landlady came around. She said that rent hadn't been paid for this month and that Nina would have to leave. She begged her to wait for her brother, just one more day, but she wouldn't listen.

By the end of the third week, Nina started to get sick. She was cold and hungry. Her clothes were now little more than rags. Nobody would even look her way. She had heard that a slavers guild kidnapped kids to sell on the black market. It would have been better than this, so she tried to sell herself to them. But they told Nina that nobody wanted a weak, sick kid about to die.

After that she retreated into a dark alley. The slums would be her grave. She curled up against a wall and her body didn't even have the energy to shiver anymore. And then there was someone standing over her; they seemed to have just stepped out of the shadows.

"I see... death... you have finally come to take me."

He didn't answer. Instead, he popped a squat and tilted his head. He seemed to be chewing on something?

"You Nina?"

Speaking was hard and she was so incredibly tired.

"Want some jerky?"

Even though she was starving she took it hesitantly before taking a small bite. It was delicious.

"So... does this mean you will stop haunting me now?"

"Haunting you? Death, does this mean even you don't want me?"

"I'm not death. So is that a yes or no?"

"Oh... well, then I will wait here for him..."

Her eyelids were getting heavy. There was no need to fight it anymore. At least she wouldn't die hungry.

"That... is not an acceptable answer."

If she stayed out here any longer, she would definitely die. However, Thistleman didn't want to take her back to the inn either. He stretched out his arm towards the wall. It has been a long time since he'd used this spell and he wasn't sure how well it would work. But, best to practice now before using it on the inn.

"Time and space, heed my call. Time, I hold thee constant, while space, I command you, provide me refuge from wind and rain, cold and heat. Open a new realm for me, one with a fire to keep me warm, space so I may sleep, and a door to keep out my enemies. Come forth, *Dimensional Tear!*"

An oozing, viscous black fluid congregated into a ball in front of Thistleman's outstretched hand, before erupting into the stone wall. A small door materialized into the side of the alley wall.

Thistleman reached down and picked the little girl up, before carrying her through the door. Inside was a very small room, no larger than eight feet wide by five feet long. It had a small fireplace in which a magical fire burned. The ceiling was low, just barely high enough for him to stand. Thistleman sighed in disappointment.

"Seems I can only do so much right now. Well, it will have to do."

He set his pouch of jerky in the corner of the room, and laid Nina down near the fire. Then, on his way out the door, and almost as an afterthought, he took his water skin and tossed it in to the corner with the jerky.

Tonight was what the townsfolk would call a lucky night. The sky was perfectly clear, and a full moon illuminated the forest. Thistleman could hear a monster fight nearby. He leapt from treetop to treetop, as silently as the wind.

Nearing the sounds of battle, he could see a huge, green troll practically swinging a whole tree at a saber-toothed tiger. Thistleman smiled to himself—troll hide would make for an excellent water skin. Also, their meat was naturally tough and considered repulsive to most species, it preserved well, and when smoked lost its acrid smell.

Except... something was wrong A saber-toothed Tiger should have been able to wipe the floor with a troll, even one this big, by leveraging its superior speed and intellect. Why was it just taking these hits?

Not that Thistleman could complain—saber-tooth hide was just as good for a water skin and their meat was more flavorful. If he gave some to Nina it could stop those dreams again for a little while.

Crunch.

The troll finally managed to land a killing blow. After breaking one of the saber-toothed tiger's legs, it took a mighty swing and crushed its skull, splattering chunks of meat and brain onto the rocky ground.

The troll looked over to his prize and stared in a stupor for a moment. Then he began salivating. Delicious, soft man meat had appeared next to the cub.

The troll bellowed as he wound up and delivered his blow. However, he didn't expect to receive a sudden shock from his club.

The human had stopped his club with his hand. His eyes... weren't human eyes. Those yellow slits filled him with fear. His club shattered and, with a crash, the troll fled through the underbrush back into the darkness of the forest.

Thistleman turned to the nearby saber-toothed tiger cub, who had been cowering from the battle as its parent was slaughtered before it. The cub had an injured leg and was mewing pathetically. Well, best to leave it then. Thistleman walked up to the cub's mother, touched it with his hand, and the space around the body began to distort before the corpse disappeared.

Far away, a yelp of shock could be heard from Nina's new room.

As Thistleman turned to walk away, the cub made a fateful decision. It tried to follow him into the forest, mewing incessantly.

Thistleman stopped and looked at the little cub limping towards him. He waited until the cub reached him. It looked up and rubbed its face against him. What a weird creature. Thistleman picked the cub up and looked into its eyes. *Now what about you is worth dying for?* He decided after much thought that the benefits of investigating this strange power outweighed the risks. How he would explain this to Diane? After much though, he came up with a plan. A devious plan, indeed.

That morning, Diane woke up to a crash from the window, and started screaming before something fluffy landed on top of her face. Thistleman stealthily warped back into the room, took a deep breath, and readied himself.

"Why, what's this?! An injured saber-toothed cub has come flying in through the window! Ahhh!"

Ah, a beautiful delivery! Who needs practice to be an actor when it can just be this easy?

Chapter 16: The Great House War

"Messenger, report!"

Duke Vermillion sat on his throne, rubbing his temple slowly, while his face was scrunched up in agonizing thought. Underneath his eyes, dark circles were forming from many sleepless nights and constant meetings with his war council.

Things were going much more poorly than he'd anticipated, and that bastard Horatio was proving to be just as wily an opponent as the rumors had suggested he would be. Shortly after he killed Asimore, he ordered all his troops near the border of Mournholm, the count's realm, to launch a surprise attack. He was aiming to take advantage of the count's preoccupation with the expedition to the Northsreach Mountains to keep him from discovering what had occurred until it was too late, and that the count would already be engaged in battle with various goblin and orc tribes, thus weakening his forces.

However, Duke Vermillion greatly underestimated Count Horatio's intelligence network. The man was considered one of the four pillars of the kingdom for a reason, and instead of launching his subjugation force into the mountains, he immediately launched it into Duke Vermillion's territory, and seized the farming village of Reims as well as the local barony, adjacent to the River Cairn which ran down the center of the kingdom. However, in a move shocking to Duke Vermillion and quite fortuitous, he stopped his forces there and had not advanced since.

Unfortunately for Count Horatio, the Culaine family was also considered another one of the four pillars of the kingdom. While he didn't have the good fortune to have a ready-made army of adventurers already recruited, he did have a large population ripe for conscription, and a massive treasury to recruit mercenaries.

The messenger was dressed in plain military fatigues, sharply pressed and with numerous accents emphasizing the red top and bright white bottoms. He kneeled with precision and lowered his head, before speaking.

"My lord, General Napolitano is reporting that our forces are ready for deployment. They are only waiting for you to take lead of the formation. We have twenty thousand peasant conscripts, five thousand soldiers from the professional garrison and, counting the Band of Medina, which has just arrived this morning, we have up to ten thousand nine hundred mercenaries."

"Excellent! Finally, some good news! Tell General Napolitano to have all troops stand by for departure. We leave the moment I arrive. Magister Hamlin, prepare my entourage! Also, send someone to Garland's chambers. Its time my son showed his abilities by acting as regent while I lead the war effort."

An older man, wearing layered black robes with long, hanging sleeves, stood up from his small desk in the corner of the room. Several other court attendants were busy transcribing notes and sifting through reports. The man bowed deeply and acknowledged the duke's request with a simple, "Yes, my lord." Then, he turned his head slightly towards one of the attendants who nodded once and hurried from the room, followed shortly after by the solemn magister.

The magister considered their adversary. Count Horatio was a man so terrifying, it may have been more apt to describe him as a hyper-intelligent monster. His skill with a blade matched his skill in magic, and both were refined to the point where he was considered peerless. The king had even tried to offer him a dukedom, then an archdukedom, but twice the count refused. Instead, he had focused on hunting monsters for the good of the realm, earning him incredible fame as a hero.

By far, though, the most unnerving part of the count was his intelligence network. He was always incredibly well informed of events throughout the kingdom, and seemed to find out things far faster than any other lord. But not one lord in the entire realm had been able to infiltrate the count's network. Every single spy sent disappeared, never to be seen again.

However, the man did have a couple of weaknesses. His army lacked in numbers and he was said to only travel at night due to his eccentricity and paranoia. Hopefully, their advanced recon team would be able to shed some more light on these tendencies and perhaps find a hole in his defenses.

Having arrived at Magus Francois's study, the magister had no more time to further reflect upon the state of the realm. Fortunately, the knight captain was also here, so it saved him a trip to the barracks. Ignoring the shouting match over strategy between the two, he readily inserted himself with the practiced grace of a longtime bureaucrat and administrator with a polite cough.

"Ahem, esteemed lords, the duke is preparing to move out. Gather your men and meet in front of the manor so his entourage may depart, posthaste. His lordship, Sir Garland, shall be managing the realm in our absence, so send your deputies to brief his team on any relevant issues before joining us outside the city. It is quite a large force, so it should be easy enough to catch up.

Archion. The nightless city.

A metropolis dwarfed only by the imperial capital of Dyrrachion, the pride of the Rivellion Empire.

Over a million people called it home, and tens of thousands inhabited the lush plains of the surrounding area that provided food for its hungry residents. Through the power of magic, the city thrived, and people were able to work night and day.

Such a massive population made housing extremely hard to manage, and numerous towers of brick and stone filled the city, crammed with residents for the sake of efficiency. The lower floors of such towers were converted into small markets, which abounded with all kinds of local delicacies and foods. The major roads were crowded with people, often avoiding speeding noble carriages like a swarm of mullet evading a predator.

To separate themselves from the peasants and lower nobility, the great and wealthy nobles of the city had recently invested incredible sums in building the floating islands which dotted the sky. Servicing these islands were the nation's first small fleets of airships, an extremely recent addition to the forces under the command of the king of Luthas, Lex Calrainne.

Such an addition was made possible only because of a theft from the forges of Moeria.

A few years ago, a young, obsessive genius arrived in one of the small local villages. He claimed to have stolen the technical readouts for dwarven airships. After some investigation, not only were they confirmed to be the genuine article, but the young man claimed he was able to construct the airships. However, it was clear that such a talent also bore the signs of lunacy. When the king asked him why he would do something as suicidal as breaking in to Moeria and stealing from the dwarves, the man simply responded, "No fantasy world should go without airships; I would gladly stake my engineering degree on it!"

Many thought the king mad for funding such a ludicrous venture, however all doubters were silenced when, a year later, the king's personal flagship ascended. It was a large ship, over fifty meters in length, with dozens of propeller engines. All of them were powered by an intricate grid of mana crystals which were attached to an orb at the helm which was used to steer the ship. The king named the vessel *Queen Anne's Revenge*.

Soon thereafter, a massive workshop rose above the skyline of the city, producing new airships at an astonishing rate. Unfortunately, the dwarves assassinated the young genius who had filched their designs before more of his ambitious projects could be unveiled. For his contributions, the king allowed him to be buried in the royal mausoleum, a tribute to the unparalleled genius of one E.K. Adams.

King Lex Calrainne mentally groaned, skillfully hiding his annoyance behind a stoic royal expression. Today he had to deal with a truly disastrous situation facing his kingdom. He was old, very old, and since his first son died as an infant, he had no heir to carry on his line. He had wanted to retire peacefully, but fate had other plans for him, and now he had to resolve a titanic issue rapidly spiraling out of control.

Before him stood Antoinette Culaine, first daughter of Duke Vermillion, and Henrik von Krauss, second son to Duke Horatio. Both had come to petition the King to sanction the other party, each one claiming the other side acted first to declare war. Unfortunately, their untimely arrival resulted in their petitions devolving into a shouting match and accusations between the two guests.

Antoinette was a gorgeous young woman and was considered a prodigy for her age. She wore a tight pink dress, with silver heels, and a glittery red bow in her hair. She had already been accepted to the prestigious University of Sangkore when she came of age in two years' time. Opposite her was Henrik, who appeared far more gaunt and pale, bearing an almost unhealthy look. He wore well-fitting dark leathers and had a short black and red cape trailing him, with an insidious looking longsword strapped to his side. In spite of his fragile appearance, he had an uncanny amount of energy.

"How dare you show your face here, scoundrels! Was murdering my brother not enough for you?"

"Hah! Murder? You think we wouldn't have found out about your assassination plans? If not for our timely discovery, my father would be dead right now!"

"Brazen lies! One look at your surprise march into our territory would reveal your insincerity!"

"A surprise march? You were clearly readying an army to invade us. We have already lost Reims to your barbaric horde!"

"Hmph, and we have not gone a step further! We are waiting in good faith to negotiate before the king!"

"Hooooo, negotiate? What is there to negotiate while you are oppressing our people! You need to return Reims to us before we can even consider negotiation!"

The king's agitation was slowly building. He was tired of dealing with this, and with all these petty, entitled nobles and their disputes. The only reason he held on was because of his younger twin brothers, both of whom claimed their son was the rightful heir to the kingdom. He was afraid his death would split the kingdom between each of them and their backers. Worse still, if he acknowledged either one as the rightful heir, he was certain it would split the kingdom anyway after his death.

The doors to the royal audience chamber were thrown open. In the midst of the chaos, a familiar pair of voices rang out in unison. "Brother, it is time we settled this issue once and for all! Make a decision. Whose son will inherit the kingdom?"

Entering the chamber were none other than Archdukes Guilford and Traxis. Both men were still imposing despite their age, and each twin was just as conniving as the other, having built a large coalition across the country. The only difference between the two was their outfits, with Traxis boldly wearing a bright cyan raiment composed of puffy accents over his arms and legs, while Guilford wore a deep crimson raiment more focused on frills and waves.

Neither Antoinette nor Henrik acknowledged the arrival of the archdukes, and continued their shouting match. The two archdukes looked at each other, and then back at the spectacle before them, each arriving at a similar conclusion. Manipulative smiles spread across their faces simultaneously.

Lex Calrainne's grip tightened immensely, slowly crushing the golden arms of his throne and exposing the whites of his knuckles. His day was about to get much, much worse.

Chapter 17:
Prelude to Disaster

"Damn it! How the hell did Vermillion get wind of my plans?"

A tall man stood on the veranda of the Barony of Reims, overlooking the River Cairn. His skin was pale only further emphasized by his black and red steel armor, layered like waves across his proud chest. Chainmail skirted down from large, sharp shoulder pauldrons to his black steel wrist guards. Behind him, a large crimson cape fluttered in the wind, adorned with the sigil of his house, a knight kneeling awaiting the rising moon. His face belied his age, appearing to be that of a twenty-six year old man with a strong jaw and profoundly blue eyes, although at this moment red hues were beginning to show through them. Other than some slightly elongated canines, his teeth could be argued to be an image of perfection. In his hand was a solitary wine glass, filled with a viscous red liquid, which he sipped on slowly.

Traces of anger coursed through his otherwise melodic voice, which at first appeared to speak to nobody in particular, until a shadow dropped from the darkness of the sky to land on the veranda.

The flicker of light showed another man, pale skinned, and dressed in the servants' robes of House Vermillion, but bearing the crest of a knight on his chest. While he usually bore an aura of arrogance about him, all vestiges of it were absent at this moment.

"Well, Asimore? Time is short. Tell me, how did Vermillion find out about you?"

"Fath—"

"*Master*. There are none around worth maintaining this... masquerade for."

The sharp rebuke silenced Asimore, who bore no hint of the blade that had pierced his throat, but was still quivering in fear before this man.

"Master Horatio, I do not believe Duke Vermillion is as perceptive as you fear. It seemed to me his target was the peasant with Diane, not I."

"Tell me... Asimore, do you question my judgement?"

Asimore dropped his head still further, shaking. "No, Master!"

"Then tell me... after he 'killed' you, what did he do?"

"He launched a surprise attack on us, Master."

"And what of Diane and the peasant?"

"He sent a bounty to a bandit group, Master."

"Then what happened to the bandits?"

"All of them... were killed, Master."

"Now then, tell me of Diane's abilities, tell me of the third daughter of Vermillion. His fifth and youngest child."

Asimore felt that his master was coming to his point, but he still couldn't quite pinpoint it. Plus, he was sure that Count Horatio already knew all this information.

"She was considered a failure at birth, Master. She couldn't even manifest a mana heart."

"Hmm, so you mean to tell me that a mere ten year old child and her peasant friend bested a group of six bandits, professional killers hired by Duke Vermillion? Or, do you think it more likely they were chattel sent by the duke to reinforce the cover of a professional agent? Acting against you directly... he was bound by noble laws; he would know better than to do such a thing. But as an accident, sending a man in secret to pose as a peasant to make this more... amenable to the prideful nobles, yes, I can see it now. A professional he knew who could so expertly dodge, that it would look so perfectly..."

The count's voice began to trail off as he looked far beyond the River Cairn, towards Versailles.

"Asimore."

"Yes, Master!"

His voice was shaking and his eyes were closed. He was prepared for the usual punishment of those who failed the count.

"There is something unusual about that... girl, this Diane. In spite of being a failure, it appears she has not only settled in Njord, but has joined the Adventurers Guild. However, there are limits to what my little birds can tell me. I am certain that Duke Vermillion is up to something."

Count Horatio's eyes narrowed before he continued, "Of my subjects, you know him and Diane best. Even if you were deceived, I hope this experience has been... educational to you. I shall offer you a chance at redemption. Go to Njord and take on a new identity. I shall offer you this chance only once."

"Yes, my Master. I shall depart immediately!"

To have received such an opportunity was so rare. This was the first time he'd ever saw the count show mercy.

Shortly after Asimore's departure, another shadow approached Count Horatio from the darkness. This one did not manifest itself, and instead floated above the veranda, blocking the count's view of the moon.

"Horatio von Krauss," it rasped, "or should I say third child of House Draculae, His Eminence, Mobius, first child of House Draculae, has called the Elder Council to session. They find your... recent actions most concerning. There is a fear that you may be risking a major break of the masquerade. They demand your immediate presence."

DAMN HIM!

That Mobius knows exactly what he was doing. The greatest thorn in the count's side; a pathetic creature trapped in the old ways.

He clearly he knows what would happen to all of my work if I were to abandon Reims now. Duke Vermillion's army is on my doorstep.

Count Horatio gritted his teeth. All his planning, all his work, all his efforts to build himself into a hero of the people, to become someone so trusted and indispensable to the kingdom... even if that plan was starting to crack before his eyes, he would rather die sticking to it than falling into cowardice and becoming like the rest of those old fools. He would need no deal with the Demon Lord Carinthus to stake his claim on the world, just wait and see!

"Tell the Council I will not be attending."

"What? You cannot refuse!"

"I only have to acknowledge Father, the rest of you... cowardly ants...!"

With a swift movement of his hands, sharp claws flew out to strike through the shadow.

"AHHHHH! You will regret thissssssss..."

The shadows blended back into the night sky. Count Horatio looked down at the river, towards Archion, before he whispered quietly to himself, "Henrik... you must not fail me here. If we can secure the backing of at least one of the brothers, the Council will be too afraid to come for me."

"Mako bean stew again? C'mooon, what kind of a stingy team leader are you? The count is paying us so much more now that the subjugation is off! Look, the other teams are even roasting meat. Why can't we get something delicious, just this once?"

Angelina ignored Boris's now nightly complaints against her choice of food. Mako beans were high in nutrients and protein, despite their lack of taste.

"We aren't having any meat, Boris, because last time we went on a quest, *you* torched the village to kill a spider. The repair costs alone cleaned out our savings, and now, we need to save up again, otherwise we won't be able to get our new members some decent gear!"

Boris himself was a native of Rivellion. He was pleasantly tanned, though fairly skinny, and his oversized robes made it appear almost as if he was a walking, talking twig. He wielded a wand and wore a silver wire headband with a single gem resting in the middle. Angelina was a former paladin of the church in Rivellion, and she wore full plate armor which she had modified with a design to her liking. She never brought up why she left the church.

The other two party members were rather new additions—a quiet red dragonkin from Ignis called Grimran (Boris couldn't tell and never asked their gender, since the last person who did got a little... crispy) who specialized in close quarters fighting. The red dragon blood ran particularly strong in him and any threat to his hoard was treated with *extreme* prejudice. Then there was a lepian. Her name was Mosey. She had long and well-toned legs with large feet and a cute face with an adorable button nose. Her long, lightly furry ears were transitioning from their summer greys to a slight white, indicating the approach of winter. To have a healer with such incredible agility as her was guaranteed to provide success to any party, as she almost never needed any protection. Furthermore, the kick of a lepian was something to be feared. Unlike Ignis, she was incredibly talkative.

All of them also wore the coveted mythril plate of the Adventurers Guild.

"Look, how was I to know that one small flare would set their huts on fire?"

"Ahhh, it was such a nice little flare too!" Mosey said. "First, you screamed so pleasantly when the spider landed on your shoulder, then the hut went WHOOSH! Then you couldn't get the spider off your shoulder and you made so much wind Then everything else went WHOOSH! Hehehe!"

"Yes, so as you can see, absolutely not my fault and unavoidable. But I am a reasonable guy, see? So I will let you off the hook tonight. But tomorrow night, you owe me some meat!"

One of Count Horatio's knights entered the encampment. The dozens gathered there quickly fell silent as he made his announcement.

"Glorious adventurers! My lord, Count Horatio, to show his sincerest thanks for your service is willing to pay you early for all your work thus far! However, the dastardly Duke Vermillion is marching on us as we speak with an army of over thirty thousand troops, expected to arrive here tomorrow. We know our numbers may be small, but with quality as high as yours, the count has a genius plan to win and bring that bastard back to the negotiating table! Any adventurers who stay for the duration of the battle will receive double their initial compensation and an additional gold coin per day in battle with the duke!"

A gold coin? A whole gold coin per day? With that much wealth, they could cover all their expenses for months and still have some fun money left over! They easily would risk their lives for less, and what about facing the duke was any different than their original plans to crush some mountain goblins and orcs?

A massive outcry of support erupted from the camp. On his veranda, an insidious smile spread across Count Horatio's face as the cries echoed up to his new castle. Everything was moving according to plan; he just needed to hold the Duke on the other side of the Cairn until nightfall tomorrow. Then, he would teach him the true meaning of fear.

Chapter 18:
Night of Blood

"FORMATION.... HAAAAALT! CAVALRY... FRONT LINE, MOVE!"

A proud general sat upon his horse adjacent to Duke Vermillion, their army gathered around a hill overlooking the River Cairn, on the other side of which they could see the Barony of Reims. So far, they had seen no movement from Count Horatio or his forces.

Duke Vermillion eyed the river carefully as his troops moved in to position. Only one large stone spanned the water with barricades just visible on the other side.

"Magus! Tell me, have you been able to find anything through scrying?"

"My lord, they have set magical barriers to counter any attempt to break through. While they are strong, given some time, perhaps a day, we can break through them."

"We will do this the old fashioned way then. Have your mages reinforce the cavalry, and then prepare for bombardment. We give them no time and we give them no quarter! ATTACK!"

"Yes, my lord!"

Magus Francois raised his staff and green light flashed in to the sky.

As the cavalry begin to rush forward, a call went up from the mages on the back line.

"Light of the goddess, Myra protect us. *Barrier!*"

"As fast as the wind, swift as thunder, grant us the speed of Apollo. *Haste!*"

"Rage overwhelming, endurance never failing, strike fear into the hearts of our enemies. *Berserk!*"

Each spell cast began to reinforce and strengthen the cavalry on the frontline. The thunderous cacophony of their hooves striking the earth reverberated across the river basin, their formation picking up a terrifying speed. Shields of energy spiraled out from the lead knights, rolling towards the forest below.

Within the forest line, Angelina watched the cavalry charge. So far, everything was going just as Count Horatio predicted.

Her role was simple. Last night, the count sent their geomancers to make a huge trench and to disguise it with mundane materials. The idea was for the enemy to focus on their anti-scrying defenses and assume they were going to buy time, and therefore egging them on into attacking. As soon as the cavalry approached, she would pull the trigger, revealing the pitfall and startling the horses. In the moment before they fell into the spiked hole, the mage line would launch a fierce barrage, weakening the cavalry's defenses so that the spikes below would finish them off.

Afterwards, their melee fighters would rush forward to clear up any survivors, before forming a phalanx round the bridge and awaiting the enemy infantry. They were to hold on as long as possible, luring in as many infantry as they could, before they retreated across the bridge.

The bridge was primed with mana bombs and would be detonated as the enemy forced their way across it and got stuck on the barricades on the other side.

The whole goal of the strategy was to buy time, as, according to the count, he had allies prepared to meet up with him at nightfall to launch an assault on the duke's flank.

In order for the plan to proceed correctly, they would have to weather the first barrage of magic from the duke's army without retaliating.

It was almost time. The enemy backline lit up with a rainbow of reds, yellows, and whites, and a powerful wind gusted down from the hillside. Then, the bombardment launched.

Lightning tore through trees, fireballs exploding and frozen spears of ice stabbing into the ground. They wavered as adventurers and knights on the front line were impaled, shocked, and melted.

"Angelina! Hit the trap now! Go!"

Boris called out to her from the hole he had been cowering in before the bombardment.

Mosey seemed entranced, watching the destruction as if it were a fireworks show.

Grimran stood tall, facing the incoming bombardment, reading the flow of attack. He dodged an Ice spear and then *tanked* a fireball. The flames licked and burst around his red scales, emphasizing his bared fangs.

"NOW!"

At Angelina's shout, Grimran charged forward, and Mosey laughed and hopped along behind him, ready to heal her front line at a moment's notice. The concealment around the trench dropped. It was the moment of truth.

Boris could hear the horses whinnying as the trench was revealed. He closed his eyes tightly.

"DAMN IT ALL! BRIMSTONE AND ROCK, DIE WITH A DROP! BURN WITH THE HATRED OF A THOUSAND SUNS. *HELLFIRE!*"

At the cost of a large amount of his mana, dark flames gathered around Boris's hands. He waited for them to coalesce before he thrust them forward at the enemy cavalry. The black fire scorched all the trees in its path, before striking the barriers in front of the faltering cavalry.

The screams from the mounted knights, with their skin and bones melting under the withering flames, created a sick song of pain and suffering.

A few bold knights leapt off their horses, and dashed furiously across the ditch. They were greeted by the onslaught of furious adventurers and frenzied knights. The mages hiding on the other side of the river began to launch their counter-bombardment, and shields were being raised across their whole line. It was too late to turn back now.

With a sputtering fury, the general commanded the main army forward. Countless peasant conscripts mixed with trained knights marched towards the Cairn.

Everything was proceeding just as the count had planned.

Deep within the Barony of Reims, Count Horatio watched the battle intently through a clear crystal ball, set atop a plush black and gold pillow atop a marble pedestal.

His vampiric father had taught him long ago the importance of the masquerade. In ages long since passed, undead had fought alongside humankind and the other races to defeat the dragons. The undead of that era were the product of mages seeking to transcend the bounds of life. Soon after the dragons were defeated, Ishtar declared the acts of those sorcerers an abomination, and she declared that they too must be exterminated to preserve the divine, along with the fey and elves who she had declared complicit in spreading such profane knowledge.

Since that moment, necromantic magic was banished and its practitioners driven underground. They had their rights stripped and were enslaved by man, or were slaughtered by the thousands at the hands of the emergent demon lords. The only reason they were able to persevere at all was due to using their magical prowess to hide themselves in the farthest reaches of the world.

As for the masquerade? It was the method developed by vampires to blend into society. Only a select few, the inquisitors of the church, actively hunted them these days. The masquerade was an unforgiving system. It forbade the use or discovery of any of their vampiric abilities before the general public. Any slip-ups were punished harshly to prevent indiscretions or investigations.

For a long time, Horatio had hated this system, but he stuck by it as he had no other choice. He had always conspired and planned for a way to change it, but he never had the willingness to take overt action. However, fifteen years ago, he found his reason.

As his face contorted at the unpleasant memories of all he'd been through, a pair of slender, soft arms slid across his shoulders and over his chest. He could smell the pleasant fragrance of cherry blossoms as her brown hair brushed against his cheek.

"Maria, my sweet Maria, what brings you down here? You know I don't want you to have to see these unsightly things."

The count turned his head and saw her deep amber eyes and brow furrowed in concern. "Even if you don't want me to see them, I can see you suffering. I can see you are in pain. Is it wrong for me to want to comfort you?"

"No, there is nothing wrong with that. Thank you, Maria."

He turned around and took her in his embrace as a resolute expression came onto his face.

He would forge his own destiny, no matter the price he had to pay. He would live together with his beloved in peace. Ishtar, the council, and the demons be damned!

Duke Vermillion glared at his generals. Each and every damn one of them, incompetent fools!

First, they lost his cavalry. Then, they marched under a withering barrage of magic fire to assault the bridge, yet they couldn't break the ranks of the adventurers for almost two hours. When finally, they forced them to retreat, he had lost nearly another thousand when the area on and around the bridge blew sky high! The hands of one of his soldiers even flew all the way to his position atop the hill and struck him in his face. Then, fearful of more traps, his magicians changed strategy to one of attrition and bombarded the enemy positions with their superior numbers. However, the enemy had the advantage of swathes of forest cover.

Now, his mages had spent most of their mana. Crossing the Cairn would have to be done the hard way. At this point, noble pride be damned, he would manage his forces *personally*.

"Tell me, are the boats ready yet!"

"Yes, my lord, but why do you insist on leading the offensive across the river in boats? We should continue to wait on this side of the river as our mages recover their mana, and strike when they are ready."

"You damned fool! This entire time, you have been playing into Horatio's hands! All his attacks, all his strategies... he is trying to hold us here as long as he can. He is up to something, and it is as clear as day!"

"But sire, boats can't hold up under a barrage of magic fire—"

"Do you mean to tell me that *our* division of mages are capable of running out of magic, but *theirs* aren't? Our sheer numbers have clearly taken their toll on them as much as us. How many of their original three thousand are left? One thousand five hundred? A thousand? We still have another twenty thousand troops, and here we are, cowering with our tails between our legs! I, for one, will not stand for it! Prepare the archers and have the mages put all their power in to shielding our forces. We strike immediately under the cover of night."

Duke Vermillion stormed out of the meeting as he returned to his carriage. It was time for him to join the battle, no longer to sit as an inspiring figurehead. A pair of squires knelt before him, and at a nod, they opened a large chest in the rear of the carriage and pulled out the fabled armor of the Culaine family. Its ornamental gold plating was reinforced by dwarven mythril and orichalcum, a prize stolen long ago from the once powerful orc tribes of the Northsreach Mountains.

To supplement it, he wielded a quicksilver blade of elvish origin. For a species despised by the gods, they sure made decent weapons.

Unbeknownst to the duke, his change in temperament would save his life this night.

As the last light of the sun faded, Count Horatio had gathered his personal court far up the Cairn.

Nearly a dozen vampires and a lich approached the river.

"Archimedes," the count said, nodding to the lich, "please halt the waters so we may cross."

The lich offered a small chuckle before acceding to the request.

"You vampires and your constraints. In all these thousands of years, you haven't figured out how to overcome such simple things like crossing running water and a little bit of sunlight?"

"The art of such ancient magic has been lost to time itself. If finding and modifying such spells were so easy, I'm sure a lich such as yourself would have figured out how to make a humanoid body without all your flesh rotting off."

"Hahaha! Feisty as always, my dear Horatio. Don't forget your end of the deal. All the bodies of the duke's men will belong to me!"

"Just make sure to wait until *after* I take the remaining adventurers away from here. As long as they believe my knights gave the soldiers a proper burial and my reputation stays intact, what you do is your business."

"This is why I like you! Such a shrewd man!"

An evil glimmer shone from Archimedes' eye sockets, filled with priceless gems and small souls screaming to be free. One such soul disappeared, feeding the Lich's evil magic. It made Horatio's skin crawl, but he had no other choice if he wanted to survive and win.

With him, he had also brought two nosferatu, vampires whose faces would give even adults nightmares. He also brought a vampire muse, whose beauty and illusion magic could sow confusion deep amongst the hearts of men, and the rest were vampire beast masters.

The plan was simple. The beast masters would call upon the forces of darkness to unleash a stream of hell and shadow hounds upon the flanks of their enemy, while Archimedes would raise the fallen soldiers of the duke to create an army and launch an assault of the dead from the rear. Once the ranks fell into confusion, the muse would use her illusion and mind magic to cause the soldiers to fall upon one another, and the nosferatu would assassinate any of the leaders who tried to restore order.

It began shortly after he boarded the boat. Duke Vermillion felt he had finally turned the tide of the battle, as boat after boat of his troops landed on the shore, driving the weary adventurers back. There was hardly any magic bombardment to affect them, and the adventurers were soon falling back in a full retreat.

But the duke's elation was short lived, as his nightmare was just about to begin. Howls, most foul and deep, began to echo across the river. Shadows of fire and flame came racing out of the hills into the flanks of his troops.

Screams of horror and agony abounded, as sharp teeth shredded flesh and bone. A cold green light began to glow in the field morgue, where their fallen were being prepared for the long rest. Flesh rotted and fell off the bone, other deceased soldiers sputtered incoherently as they choked out a wail through their blood-filled lungs. Soon, the army of the dead was descending from the rear, over ten thousand strong and counting.

Incorporeal visions flitted about, friends turning into horrible monsters astride each other. Terrible monsters, diving from the black night sky, grabbing any who dared resist and carrying them into the deep darkness, only for a rain of blood and guts to fall below.

"What in the damned hell?"

Duke Vermillion, for the first time in an age, felt fear as a dark cloud descended on his army.

"Sail down river!"

A timely command, as other boats slower to launch were sunk beneath the weight of the surging bodies. This didn't stop screaming soldiers from leaping into the waters and grabbing at the side of his boat.

"Don't hesitate, cut down any who are holding us back!"

With a swift swing of his sword, fingers, arms, and hands were cleaved from the side, blood filling the river as his men sank below the darkened waters.

As the darkness began to drift across the river, Duke Vermillion could see a shadow, slicing through the wall of bodies and scattering a rain of blood on the water. A pair of cold eyes met his, those of a hunter who had found his prey.

Without hesitation, Duke Vermillion launched his most powerful spell.

"Fire, raging hot as the sun, fierce as the flow of earth, I call upon thee to smite my foes! *Eruption!*"

"Darkness eternal, shadows of night who disappear into the void, rend my foes and leave only ash. *Dark Impulse!*"

A raging white and red ball of flame and magma.

A sphere of darkness from which no light could escape.

They collided above the river, the resounding explosion toppling the remaining trees near the shore and whipping the river into a furious froth, capsizing, shattering, and sinking all the unfortunate boats too close to the epicenter. Horatio took the brunt of the blast, preventing him from chasing down Vermillion.

As each of the king's brothers backed the other contender in the war, it would soon devolve into a bloody proxy war of attrition that would bring devastation and famine across the kingdom for the years to come.

Chapter 19:
A Demon's Solution
to the Orphan problem

"Are you crazy? How can we keep it? That's a wild animal you have there! And a nasty one at that! Haven't you ever heard of saber-toothed tigers before? Don't you know how dangerous they are?!"

Ryme was in a frenzy. After the sound of the smashing window and Diane's yell, she came rushing into the room, only to find the cub on Diane's bed. Worse still, the little girl had completely attached herself to it. It was only a cub, but it was at least half her size.

"Auntie! Look what I found! Isn't he the cutest? Can we keep Clover?"

She could not let this happen, but Diane's stubbornness, while endearing, would mean that Ryme needed an ally. She glanced quickly at Thistleman, before immediately ruling him out. The kid was staring fascinated at Diane and the cub, almost excited even. That left Jotuun.

"Hey, Jotuun! We cannot raise an animal like that in this household, right? We don't even know where it came from! We should just turn it in to the Adventurers Guild or the city guard and be rid of it."

"What? No, Auntie! We can't do that. They will kill it!" Tears erupted from Diane's eyes as she clutched the furry cub closer.

Ryme looked over to Jotuun for support, but instead he said, "Hmmm. Fine. You raise though. Need new window glass, and to find pet bed."

Ryme balled her fists, her fur bristling as she turned and followed Jotuun down the hall.

"Jotuuuuuuuuun! Come back here! I am not done with you yet!"

In the meantime, Thistleman was watching in absolute *awe*. This cub's powers were *amazing!* Without using any magic at all, it had not only swayed Diane instantly, but through her, even convinced Jotuun to let them keep it. This development certainly warranted further study. If, at the very least, he could secure the cub's loyalty to him and Diane... what it did to anyone else was hardly a concern. This creature had so much potential. Thistleman grinned almost from ear to ear at the implications.

First and foremost, however, Thistleman had to deal with the Nina problem. As more of his powers returned to him, Thistleman began searching the depths of his mind. In spite of having severed his connection to the God of Darkness, there were vast portions of his memories he could not reach. How long would this portion of his mind remain locked? Why was it locked?

As he continued leaping from tree to tree, his path eventually brought him back towards Brownrock Mountain. As he began to approach, he stopped suddenly and hid his presence.

He *felt* something... something familiar. Wasn't this where he had released his miasma weeks before? Looking around, he could see that the trees and plants in the area had taken on a strange hue.

He proceeded slowly, advancing with the utmost care and not making a single sound until he reached the edge of the forest.

He could clearly see someone sitting on the edge of one of the caves that made up the hornet's former nest—humanoid in shape and of a fairly large in stature. It was clothed in various animal furs, with red and black hued skin covering an extraordinarily well built body. On his arms were two patches of shallow exposed bone, providing some armor, and on his head were two small horns indicative of his youth. Most telling, though, were his yellow eyes with his pupil slit like a cats.

It was a demon. He had inadvertently created it with his miasma.

Upon seeing Thistleman, the demon's eyes widened. It dropped from the cave entrance and immediately kneeled.

"Master! It is you! Only you could have brought me into this world! I have been feeling so lost... almost as if I have no purpose. Please, tell me! How can I serve you?"

The creature's attitude was... surprising. It was nothing like a daemon's, who would only acknowledge the power of a superior while they schemed behind their back. This was an absolute, undying loyalty. If his connection to the God of Darkness had not been broken, would he, too, be like this demon? Well, if this was a servant of his, best to test its knowledge and usefulness.

"Before that, tell me how much knowledge were you born with? I see speech was granted to you. You share the same language as I, but tell me, do you know of the common tongue here?"

"Master, from what I can recall, I know of the language and cultural norms you had at the time you graciously bestowed life upon me. Unfortunately, I only know a little of the common tongue, but that can surely be improved with study. I wish I could do more, but this is all I have for now."

"Indeed. The skills you have now are more than enough for my purpose. My hands... are quite full at the moment. I have much work to do and, unfortunately, it is frustrating having to continue dealing with all these *problematic orphans*. One is all I care to deal with."

"I see, so Master, how do you wish for me to deal with this problem for you? Shall I eradicate them?"

"No! Absolutely not! I cannot..." He almost admitted he could not risk being plagued by nightmares. What daemon would ever openly admit their weaknesses? "Ahem. I cannot allow that course of action. Feeding, housing, and raising is what I require from you. I shan't deal with her any longer. As I said, you already have the knowledge and skills; you figure out the rest and you deal with it. That shall be your duty."

"Yes, I understand, Master. I shall fulfill your will to my utmost ability!"

"Very well, then I shall call forth the one occupying my hands right now. She shall be in your care. Do not fail me. Realm of Space, I command thee, open a door and heed my will. *Gate!*"

A large, ornate door began to form in the space above Thistleman's raised hand, and as it opened, Nina feel out of it and into Thistleman's outstretched arm.

"Aieee! Oh, Death, it is you. Is it time for me to pass on yet?"

"I keep telling you, I am not Death. Your time with me is over. Now, you shall be staying with..."

The kneeling demon looked up at Thistleman expectantly. Did it even have a name? Actually... he would name the creature and it would likely just accept it.

"Yes, you shall be staying with Orion. Work diligently, eat, live, and grow well and perhaps you shall be rewarded."

"Could my reward be seeing my brother again, oh Death?"

Thistleman decided not to answer that question. He'd already decided the girl wouldn't be his problem anymore. He left, disappearing back into the darkness of the forest.

The girl turned to look at Orion.

"If you serve Death, then you must be one of his reapers. Do we have a house to stay in?"

"A house? I haven't made one... no."

"Then we need a house. He told me to work diligently for him. Maybe if I become a reaper like you, I can see my brother again?"

Orion found Thistleman's instructions vague. *He wants me to take care of her for him?* He even instructed her to work hard and, most importantly, she said it was to become a reaper like him. His master wanted an army. He wants killers. And, he wants to make them from orphans. A malicious smile spread across Orion's face. To train an army for his master. What an honor! What a responsibility! To teach these kids the demon way. It was truly a great task!

"Yes, we shall start with a house, and then a training ground. There is much work to be done, new recruit. Master is sure to reward those who don't disappoint him. Then, we shall find the rest of the members to make up your team. If there are enough, we can make even more teams."

Given time, this area had all the resources he would need.

Amala readjusted her pack, all that was left of her team's valuables as well as their remaining food from the cave. It was frustrating trying to balance it on her shoulder, and she still was not used to using only her left hand yet, and her bandaged shoulder was still aching.

She was traveling south, looking to put her past life in Njord behind her. However, having been a bandit meant that it would be hard to find work in a normal city. Considering how well the kingdom maintained an information network between cities, it would only be a matter of time until she was found out. Instead, she was looking for a small town to start over. A quiet place, one where they might be willing to accept a pretty girl with a sad story and not ask too many questions.

After a while of searching, and asking various travelers about towns and places they had visited, she found one that perfectly suited her taste. It was much further to the south, in the territory adjacent to Archduke Guilford's territory and one of the seven city states, Moxis. She couldn't remember the name of the marquis who ran the territory, but the village of Mist Vale was located along the river Cairn and wasn't too far from the sea. Even if things turned for the worse there, she could make a last ditch attempt to escape to the Treacherous Isles and join a pirate crew there.

Just this once, though, she would make an attempt at an honest living!

She smiled sadly to herself, and wondered about how different things could have turned out if she had made better decisions in life. Perhaps Gus wouldn't have died. Maybe she could have had a family? The answer to these questions, she would never know.

Chapter 20:
The Art of Darkness

Kurstwood. One week after Diane's departure from Versailles

The stone crunched under the impact of Lieutenant Septimus's boots as he dismounted his horse in the center of the village. His knights were returning from quickly scouting around the perimeter. Septimus looked around, taking in the scene before him, his eyes pouring over every detail in the midday sun.

One of his team leaders, Sergeant Alain Dufount, approached. "Sir, we have concluded that there are no hostile creatures left in the village This had to be the work of that *thing* that came through during the summoning ritual." The knight shuddered in disgust.

"So it would seem. However, some things do not match up here. Tell me, Alain, were you able to find any bodies? Or any other creatures at all?"

Alain looked over at Hal's slowly rotting corpse, and then to the remains of the other two knights within the circle of the village square.

"Other than the ones here… no. Actually, now that you mention it, the fact that these bodies were left untouched is also quite strange."

"It is indeed. Do you remember the girl's report back in Versailles?"

"No, sir. I may have forgotten."

"One weeks' liberty deducted for drinking instead of reading the report. You are a professional knight, here on an investigation from His Majesty himself."

Sergeant Alain grimaced and hung his head in shame. "Yes, sir."

"For your refresher, this is where her team fought the demon, as she called it."

"Well, that makes sense of all this devastation"

"Does it? A demon that would have cleared out the entire rest of the village, and yet left the rest of these bodies here unscathed? Look, are you telling me that this crater matches up with the destruction of the rest of the village? Then compare the blood stains themselves— you can see where the sheering of the rock has cut through the old, dried blood. But the fresh blood has poured over the edge of the crater and hardened."

Alain tried to swallow, as his throat started to turn dry. He knew the lieutenant was sharp, but he had picked up this much information without even using his magic skills.

"Now then, let's get a better look, shall we? History, unveil your secrets to me, let neither light nor shadow impair my search. *Trace!*"

Septimus's eyes opened wide. Everything he was looking for, it was here! Even after a week… so much residue of dark, demonic energy. It came from near the fountain, near the tracks of the carriage. Then, another cluster, a little farther from the carriage. It looked just like the energy called from the summoning ritual. Then, following the path to the crater, he saw something... interesting. The residue of a different demon. However, only the footprints were there, and at first it seemed like a determined advance before it ran. Clearly it did not make it very far before it got caught up and taken into whatever made that blast. That girl, and her stupid father! More must have happened than she'd let on. Even then... for a demon from Ebenheim to have come all the way out here... his investigation was only beginning.

Upon returning to Versailles, he found that the duke and his men had already begun to march to war. His knights asked around the town, trying to find where the daughter of Vermillion went, and they were able to confirm that she had gone to Archion to see the king.

Unfortunately, it led him to the wrong daughter of Duke Vermillion—Antoinette Culaine. By this time, the war between the houses was entering full swing and Diane's trail had long gone cold.

Stanley had always been a man of conscience, albeit a little lazy and not the brightest person. He was absolutely plain in every respect, with a face that was easily lost in the crowd. His lack of talent had kept him stuck in a dead end office job for most of his life, answering phones, sorting papers, reading papers, and sending summaries of those papers to people who would summarize them again, before sending them to someone else to proofread and finally deliver them to the person who would make a decision on them.

Such a life would turn any man to drinking. Eventually, one night he drank too much and hit the road, and the last thing he remembered was swerving off the road. Next thing he knew, he woke up in Anastasia.

When he first wandered into the town of magic, he was absolutely ecstatic, having read stories of great adventure all his life. Soon, he would learn, the stories were just that... pleasantries to help the masses escape the pain of their reality. Here, all he found was suffering, and then more suffering. He couldn't speak to anyone, and the work was grueling.

He then tried to become an adventurer, but there he learned he was not special. Others used him, treated him as nothing more than a meat shield or baggage carrier. By then, he had finally learned enough of the language to get by. That is when he found a job recruitment poster. 'Njord Adventurer's Guild is hiring! Office worker positions available! Safe, dull work environment filing paperwork and submitting reports.'

It was a dream come true. Something he knew how to do, a way to escape the roughness of everyday life. So he took the job. For a while, it was great. He had everything he wanted. At least, that was until he started noticing something strange happening. Ever since that girl Diane arrived, data he compiled was reviewed, and a lot of key things from it went missing. He started making some secret copies, just to make sure he wasn't crazy, and started seeing that the information reported was... adjusted. Then, there were the demographic reports sent by the city guard. Apparently, there were some small reports about less orphans being found around town. However, nobody pressed to much about it, but once reaching the guild, at the very least an investigation quest should have been issued. Instead, those reports just... disappeared.

Then, he started to notice another trail. People who had asked questions about it... disappeared. But eventually, their death reports disappeared from the records or were also adjusted. Something was up, someone was hiding something. Stanley knew it had to be someone important in the guild, so he decided to take his compiled documents and try to sneak out of the city with them. He had to get his reports to the guild master!

"Ah, quite a pleasant night for a walk, isn't it, Stanley?"

The guards on the south gate had fortunately been sleeping, so he had slipped quietly past them. However, he had not expected to run in to the branch manager in the middle of the road.

"Do you know how long ago it was I came to this world?"

Stanley kept silent. He noticed that, for some reason, the branch manager was holding a small package of meat.

"Fifteen years ago today, if I recall right. At the time, I was summoned by a very sad little man with big dreams. Mr. Eric von Straught, he begged me to help him become a branch manager in the Adventurers Guild! I could hardly believe it, such a scrawny and pathetic man, with dreams far too big for himself!"

Stanley did not like where this was going. He did not like it at all.

"But then... he told me, he was willing to offer anything to be able to make it here. Now that is something I would have to be... *heartless* to refuse. Ahaahaha!"

Sheer malice radiated from Baal as he continued his speech.

"Then, just as I was getting bored, worried I was missing out on all the fun back home, something *interesting* came to me. A little girl, determined to be an adventurer. That on its own is not much, but here is the kicker—she was originally a failure with no future, who was contracted to *none other than my master!* Can you believe it? I have so much I want to say to him, so much I want to *know!* But there is an iron law where I come from, passed down from my oldest ancestors after their birth, and the only demons to have ever spoken with Dagon himself. His instructions were simple—to build a nation worthy of him, and that from that moment on, they were to never disturb him in his room. Any who did, he promised, would certainly die by his hand without thought or mercy. Now, do you know why I am telling you this, Stanley?"

"B-b-b-because you're going to kill me?"

"Wrong! Well, half wrong. You *are* still going to die. Hehehe, well, have fun, my dear Stanley. This is why I like recruiting your kind to work for me, you always know just enough to keep things fun for me!"

As he spoke those last words, Baal removed his hood, revealing two thick horns curling over his head, much like those of a bull. His black and red skin and infernal smile were revealed. Stanley began to realize that the entire time, the robe was magically enchanted to make it appear as if there was human face underneath the hood.

As Baal faded into the darkness, Stanley could hear the growls coming closer, and numerous pairs of large, bloodthirsty eyes began to emerge from the darkness, with snouts full of razor sharp teeth and bodies the size of horses.

He realized what the meat was for, too. Dire wolves could follow the smell of blood from miles away. Stanley glanced back at the town, much too far away. The guards sleeping made sense now. From the moment he started gathering documents, he was a dead man. He closed his eyes and turned his face towards the sky. If this was to be his fate, at least he would accept it peacefully.

Thistleman had been preparing his book for months now, and he was certain that it was ready for Diane. He wasn't sure how fast she would pick up the skills, but if needed, he could just make another book later. He decided to pack in a few of the essentials, basics to help any demon get by in the world. Could a human learn demon skills? Well... that was another thing he had to find out.

He had described six different skills, illustrated with the best artwork he was capable of. At their most basic, their benefits were decent but nothing spectacular. However, once they were fully mastered, each of these skills could become quite terrifying. Diane already gained access to *Demon Sight* and *Demonic Fury* through the nature of the contract and her own temperament. Gaining these additional skills would be much harder. The skills he planned for her were *Shadow Step, Demonic Resistance, Infusion, Devour Life, Devil's Ray,* and *Concealment*.

Shadow Step used mana to improve speed. It could also be used to move between areas of darkness and shadow. *Demonic Resistance* was much simpler in comparison, as that one simply involved using a demonic aura to reinforce the skin to protect from blows.

Then there was *Infusion* which involved assigning elemental magic properties to weapons and armor. This skill was highly draining in terms of mana usage. While contracted to Thistleman, Diane would be able to use the skill for far longer than most other adventurers.

Devour Life drained the energy or soul of the target, but the hard part there would be convincing Diane to change her mindset to agree to wield the skill.

Last were *Devil's Ray* and *Concealment*. *Devil's Ray* delivered a powerful, precision blast of dark energy and *Concealment* used mana to diffuse light around the caster. At the higher levels, *Concealment* could turn the user completely invisible.

Now, for the hard part—making sure that Diane discovered the book in a believable way. After some careful thought, and checking the guild quest boards, he was eventually able to come up with a suitable solution. First, he needed to acquire a treasure chest. Then, he would need to manually age it a bit, before slipping it into an ogre cave. Well, it ought to work. From what he had overheard in his short stay in Njord so far, adventurers rarely questioned what they found in such places. Now how to point Diane in the right direction...

Chapter 21: The Hunt Begins

'In such a diverse world as ours, it is important for all our students to learn the difference between a skill and a spell, as well as the importance of quick casting. A skill uses relatively little mana but is heavy on stamina, and can be cast immediately and repeatedly. However, skills can only be learned through repeated training, thus are most commonly found among the soldiers and adventurers of each nation.

Spells, on the other hand, are a much higher art and are learned from the experience and wisdom of our forebears. Access to such tomes of wisdom is a pursuit best left to the nobles who can attend our academy. They can be cast in two forms—full spells for maximum power and efficiency of mana, or quick casting at a much weaker potency. If possible, mages want to avoid quick casting except in emergencies in order to best preserve their mana and to get the maximum effect.'

–Archmage Tyrus the Bold, founder of the University of Sankore, deceased

"Hrmmmmm...."

Thistleman was musing to himself, while playing around with different illustration of people using the *Greater Illusion* spell. Getting Diane to take the ogre quest was one thing, but not getting her killed in the process of retrieving the book was another thing altogether. Ogres are tougher monsters, so she would need some meat shields, and with the bulk of high tier adventurers gone for the copious well-paid mercenary missions, not many of the remaining decent adventurers wanted to hunt an ogre.

Now how to acquire said meat shields without using some form of mind control? The main issue was that while *Greater Illusion* could replicate sounds, and do a fantastic job at making an illusion look real, it lacked, however, corporeality, which could cause problems. Ah, what a headache.

Then, inspiration struck. What if he could make another demon? It has been a little while since the incident with the hornets, and enough of his miasma had regenerated... although testing this in the city would be troublesome.

It was time, therefore, to make a quick trip to the forest.

Now for a deep breath. He only had enough miasma to try this once. *Focus. Absolute focus.* Keeping the image of what he wanted to achieve clear in his head, the miasma poured in an uncontrolled manner.

"Damnit! This is harder than I thought! I need to focus!"

The process wasn't perfect, but it started to work. Soon, a soft white hand began to form and reach out through the mist, then a slender arm rapidly condensing behind, followed by a soft and curvy torso, with long, firm legs. And a tail. And black wings. Thistleman started getting a little worried, but he tried to maintain his focus. Then, her face... a beautiful woman's face, and long ears and small horns. Damnit.

" Master! Thank you for calling me into this world! I am ready to follow your... ah... every order!"

She made a very clear attempt to look vulnerable, before she was hit in the face by a kimono.

"Get dressed. I have a very special job for you, as I am sure you already know."

"Do you have a name for me, Master?"

"Yes, you shall be called Sayomi."

Thistleman sighed as Sayomi finished getting dressed. It seemed that he would be running through a few more copper and bronze quests with Diane before he could get her to his book. Her growth was not going to go anywhere near as quickly as he hoped. Ah, may as well clear this excess miasma now too. He didn't want to warp these trees and leave evidence behind.

Forged in Fire

This morning, I woke up just brimming with energy! Even though it was a cold winter morning, today was looking like a wonderful day! The sun was out and I was ready to take on my day.

I was terrified when I first came here. Looking back at everything, if Thistle wasn't with me the whole time, I probably would have given up a long time ago, and I definitely wouldn't have made it this far.

I put a lot on him, and to be honest, I feel a little bad about it, but I am trying my best too! Every chance I get, I am taking on new quests. After all, I need to earn my keep! Plus, seeing how scary things are out there, I know I need to get stronger.

Today, though, I feel motivated to take on a new challenge! Should I try for an Iron Plate quest? My new Copper rank has given me a lot more sway, and Elsie seems to recognize me a lot more when I am in the guild now! She is even treating me nice. Maybe when I get a little richer and more famous I can hire her to make Thistle's life a little easier.

Thistle still isn't awake yet? That sleepyhead! Alright, I suppose he has earned friendship rights by now. I don't have to always act like a noble around him.

"Thistle! Wakey wakey, sleepyhead!! Come on! It's time for breakfast and we need to get another quest today!"

"Mmmhhmm... it's that time again? Ughhhh.... Alright, alright! I'm up, you don't have to drag me by my hair!"

Diane quickly dressed in her usual purple dress, now with many more stitches than before, and hurried down the stairs for breakfast. After scarfing down eggs and toast, she ran out the door with a second piece of toast in her mouth. She waved to Ryme and Jotuun, who smiled and waved back to her as the door swished shut behind her.

She was so focused on getting to the guild that she didn't notice Thistleman giving a small thumbs-up to someone after the door closed behind him.

What used to be a bustling guild hall now only had a few copper and bronze plate teams, with some independent iron and bronze plated adventurers and a silver plate team.

I gave Elsie a nice wave as I ran up to look at the quest board.

"Nyah! Welcome byack, Miss Diane."

"Morning Elsie."

As I was looking at the quest board, Thistle walked up beside me, giving the quests a good look over himself. He always asked me about a bunch of them.

"Hey Diane, what do you think about this one? It says something about some ogres?"

"Ogres? Well, I was wanting to try something a bit harder, like maybe an iron plate quest... but that one is a silver plate full party quest. I'm not sure I would want to..."

At that moment, the door to the adventurer's guild swung open, and a desperate cry filled the room.

"Someone... anyone... please, help me! Some ogres tried to kidnap me while I was picking berries in the forest, but when my brother came to protect me, they took him instead! I beg of you, can someone save my brother? I will do *anything*, so please... help me!"

A beautiful woman had entered the guild, her eyes were full of tears and her torn and disheveled clothes emanated desperation. The guild quickly filled with noise. While the copper and bronze plate teams shared looks of fear, the silver plate team stood up and approached the woman, with their only female member trying to slow them down.

"Miss, we are the Avengers of the Dawn, and we will gladly help you save your brother in your time of need! My name is Gungnir, I am the team leader and a former knight, and these three with me are Efrain, our sorcerer, Fido, a magic swordsman, and Emily, our ranger! You are safe with us. Please, what is your name? And where do you need us to go?"

Efrain was a surprisingly muscular man for being a sorcerer and he carried a short sword. Fido was a wolf canian who used a two-handed claymore embedded with a single mana crystal to improve mana flow. Emily

205

was a tall, plain-faced woman in green leather armor with a long bow and miniature crossbow at her side. She also wore a green cap which she kept all the way down, completely over her ears.

"Gungnir, stop! Think about this for a second! These are ogres we are talking about. We don't even have a healer or a scout or even a porter. If we wait for Mythrandir's team to get in, I am sure I can talk to him and Terra to get their support. This is too risky!" Emily said.

"Emily, every moment we wait, we risk the death of her brother! No man can allow a lady to suffer so!"

"Ahem! Excuse me? But I was looking at the ogre subjugation quest first, you all better not be thinking about stealing it from me!"

The nerve of these people! Even if I wasn't sure I wanted to take the quest, the fact I was looking at it first meant I should have first rights to it. That is just common courtesy!

"Ruff, I see, you're the little missy always causing a stir around here," Fido said. "This is no place for a Copper. Let us men handle it!"

"Ah, but didn't you say you needed a porter? Her and her friend are pretty small, but looking at his pack, they can definitely carry things for you. Please, my brother's life is at stake!"

The woman took hold of Gungnir's hand and leaned in closely with tears in her eyes. The view was too perfect. He blushed.

"No worries, we will definitely save him! But still, I am not sure about these kids, and Silver is the minimum requirement for this quest."

As they were discussing the problems, Haraldr, now wearing a newly minted bronze plate, came running up to the group.

"Did I hear you needed a scout? I was the rogue for my... old team, and as long as it isn't fighting the ogres, I can at least guarantee my ability to sneak and report to you!"

He subtly gave Diane a thumbs-up and a wink.

During these discussions, a robed and hooded man approached Elsie, before leaning to her ear and tapping on her shoulder, then walking away.

Elsie jumped with a look of shock on her face, and then ran to the group.

"Nyah! There is nyo worry about her plyate, she is a special cyopper, her and her friends are allowed for this request!"

"What? She is a special rank?! Really? I wonder what her skills are like."

The group of silver plates stepped back in shock, before their sorcerer, Efrain, spoke to her.

"She is definitely good, I can vouch for that. She managed to take out a giant hornet nest after all, and even escaped from dire wolves!"

"In my entire career, I have only heard about special ranks from other city guilds," Efrain said. "I would love to see one in action."

"Then it is settled! You have your porter and a scout, so now we can go save my brother! Oh, by the way, my name is Sayomi. I will be in your care."

The way she batted her eyelids, the male adventurers couldn't help but follow her out of the guild, accompanied by the jealous stares of the lower ranked adventurers. The only person who was showing any apprehension at the current chain of events was Emily, but she wouldn't abandon her team. They had been through too much together. She could only hope that her intuition was wrong.

It was a bit of a hike until we reached the ogres' cave. Thankfully, we were able to make it there without much incident. Although it was cold, like getting really cold. I definitely needed to ask Thistle to buy me some winter furs when we get back in to town!

The whole time Sayomi seemed so scared that the men just kept doing all they could to comfort her. The only ones who weren't caught up over her were Emily and Thistle, which is probably why we ended up being our own little clique.

Apparently, Emily had been part of this group for a few years, and they had gone from Copper to Silver in a decent amount of time. Their party had never hunted down ogres before, but they had lots of experience with all manner of other creatures. Emily wouldn't say where she was from, but I started to notice that she seemed... really light, and her features seemed more refined than a normal person's. Was it just me, or had my eyes been getting sharper?

We were able to identify the lair well before we reached it, due to the nasty smell. We had Haraldr sneak up to confirm it, and outside were various bones and piles of... filth. Sayomi also spotted a small beaded bracelet in the bushes, and she tearfully insisted it was her brother's. This really seemed to whip up the men.

We had Haraldr move ahead of our group, while we followed shortly behind. He seemed proud of his new spell–*Concealment*. With the help of the darkness, it made him almost disappear!

Inside the cave, the smell of rotten flesh was overwhelming. The silence within was broken only by the drip drip drop of water falling from the stalactites. After what felt like an eternity creeping through the darkness,

Haraldr quietly hustled back to the group. He spoke in a hushed yet urgent whisper.

"I found them! Three ogres are currently eating something in the room ahead."

"Ruff. Are they armed?"

"Two wooden clubs and one crude stone axe. There was one standing at a large table while another was tending a pot over the fire. The one with the axe is sitting by the wall on the far side."

"Then a quick ambush may be our best bet," Gungnir said. "Kill them before they can call for help."

"I don't like this," Emily said. "Maybe we should find a way around to get Sayomi's brother and just get out before they notice us?"

"You know, she might be right," Thistleman said. "You can never be too careful around here."

"We don't even know where the other paths lead, and if Haraldr is right, we don't have time! They might begin to cook him before we can find a way around," Efrain said.

"Also, do we want to risk alerting other ogres," Thistleman said. "What if this isn't all of them?"

"No, we strike now, hard and fast. Efrain, take the far ogre with one of your spells. Emily, assist him. I will go for the ogre at the table. Haraldr, stand back as support for me. Fido, you go for the ogre by the cooking pot with Diane as support. We are the Avengers of the Dawn!"

We stealthily moved to the entrance of the chamber and Gungnir gave the signal.

The speed with which he and Fido stormed forward took me by surprise, and it took everything I had to keep up with Fido. The front ogres hardly had any time to react!

"*Shield of Stone! Bull's Rush!*" cried Gungnir.

"*Bestial Fury! Lion Strike*!" bellowed Fido.

"Chains of steel, born of magic to bind my foes, I call upon thee! Bind Monster!" Efrain called as he wielded his magic.

"May the spirits of nature guide my arrow," Emily said, "strike true with the guidance of the wind! *Elemental Arrow!*"

I felt excitement coursing through my veins. I couldn't wait to show off some of my abilities too! However, I failed to notice something I had not seen in a long time… a look of concern on Thistle's face. He kept looking back at the path we came from.

Chapter 22:
A Painful Lesson

Each of the ogre's brothers lay in a pool of their own blood; the surprise attack had proven effective thus far. However, the instinct of a creature in danger is nothing to scoff at. As soon as the magical chains erupted from the ground, the ogre strained to fight against them. It saw the arrow coming for its throat and, at that moment, dropped his chin and crushed the arrow with his teeth. The wind reinforcement burst from his mouth with a furious gust!

"I can't hold him anymore. Hurry and finish him off!" Efrain shouted

The magic chains binding the ogre creaked furiously under the creature's strength, before snapping and disintegrating into the mana from whence they came.

The ogre roared, towering nine feet over them.

"I will hold its attention!" Gungnir shouted. "Everyone, focus it down and attack! *Bull's Rush!*"

The ogre trembled with rage as it reached over and grabbed its large stone axe. A red aura began to emanate from the creature.

"Shit! It's going berserk!"

"YOU! KILL! AVENGE! FAMILY!"

The axe collided with Gungnir's shield, shattering it and flinging him nearly all the way across the room.

"AWOOOOOO! *LION STRIKE!*"

With a leap, Fido's claymore struck with a vicious fury towards the exposed throat of the rampaging creature. However, it was faster. *Much faster.* With a supernatural fury, it twisted its head to lock eyes on Fido, and punched him in the chest with the force of a cannon. The canian was sent flying back towards the cooking pot as blood sprayed from his mouth.

Diane quickly changed her trajectory. She dodged to the side just as the ogre brought its axe crashing to the floor. A moment later and she would have been crushed. She quickly rolled backwards, dodging another brutal blow.

"*Fireball!*"

The ogre was struck by the fierce explosion to its chest and took a step back, before leaning forward through the flames and roaring.

"*Grease!*" Efrain launched a quick cast spell to throw the ogre further off balance, "Emily, Gungnir, now!"

Emily quickly launched a series of arrows at the ogre, one of which pierced the creature's eye.

With his left arm dangling by his side, Gungnir drew his longsword and blitzed towards the blinded creature, dodging a wild swing before piercing its throat, unleashing a fountain of blood.

The creature's body crashed to the floor.

"That... was just one?" *Huff.* "I hate to think what would happen if we hadn't surprised the others."

"Damn, Sayomi," Gungnir said, "if there are more, we might not be able to save your brother." [Gungnir]

"W-what? But we have already come this far. We can't leave him now!"

In the meantime, Thistleman hurriedly slipped to his chest stashed in the corner of the room and took a seat with an audible sigh.

"Hmm? Hey Thistle, what are you sitting on there? Is that a chest?"

"Eh, what? This?"

"No, that's definitely a chest! C'mon, let me open it!"

As Diane opened the chest, Efrain's eyes went wide.

"Careful with that! What if it's trapped?"

Inside the chest was a single tome, bound in beast leather and imprinted with a skull. Its clasp was sealed with bone, and a dark energy seemed to almost pour from its pages.

"This energy... this book clearly isn't safe." Efrain boldly tried to slip his hand in to snatch the book, his eyes filled with greed, but Diane was quicker.

"Hey! Finders keepers! If this book is so dangerous, then why are you trying to grab it?"

"I am an experienced mage!"

"Come now, girl, you should trust him," Gungnir said. "Efrain has always been a good ally and friend! As party leader, it is my duty to ensure rewards are adequately distributed! Just give up the book."

"Hey guys, now shouldn't be the time to be arguing! I can hear something coming down the hallway. A lot of something!"

The chorus of howls echoing throughout the cavern sent shivers down everyone's spine. They had charged in to the belly of the beast without a full team and unprepared, and now they were going to suffer for it. All thought of the book dropped out of Gungnir and Efrain's minds as they prepared themselves for what was to come.

Thistleman was furious. His plan to get a team into the ogre dungeon had been too successful. These idiots had lost a hold of their senses and put everything at risk. Now, that risk was bearing down on Diane.

Sayomi ran back behind Gungnir as Emily fired an arrow down the hall, before she too turned to run. An ogre burst into the cavern and swung faster than she could react. With a sickening *thunk*, Emily was sent flying into a wall and dropped to the ground, unconscious. Haraldr disappeared back in to the shadows, clearly shaking in fear. Another ogre charged in to the room, and then another.

"Thistle, don't worry about me!" Diane shouted. "Grab Emily and get out of here!"

Gungnir and Fido locked eyes with each other, before turning to charge at the ogres. Diane launches another fireball, but they continue to charge right through it as if it is nothing more than a nuisance.

The sound of Fido's ribs breaking could be clearly heard.

Gungnir was knocked out cold.

Efrain shrieked before fainting in fear. The only ones left now were Diane, Sayomi, and Thistleman.

Thistleman looked at Sayomi and pointed to Emily's limp body, and she nodded.

Diane used her magic to maximize her speed. She dodged a titanic fist and leaped towards the wall before flipping around, her feet landing on the side and her legs fully squatting. She launched towards the nearest charging ogre, pouring all her mana into her rapier as she stabbed in to its eye!

The creature screamed and thrashed in its death throes, collapsing in a tower of muscle.

And, right over top of it, a stone sledge flew in and struck Diane in the side with a resounding *crack*. Terror and pain were the last expressions on her face before she was knocked out cold.

As the ogres charged towards Thistleman and Sayomi, they stumbled, then shrieked in surprise. Both of them had disappeared right before their eyes. Most shocked of all, was the ogre that reached down to grab Diane's body, which lay like a bloodied rag, only to have his fist bounce off the floor. His hands grabbed nothing at all.

Outside the cave, Thistleman was furious.

"GOD DAMN IT ALL! DAMN THESE FUCKING OGRES! DAMN THESE USELESS SILVERS!"

The earth shook a little as Sayomi set Emily down.

"But we were able to get her your book," she said. "Even if it didn't all go according to plan, in the end, it still worked out, Master! They are just some small injuries anyways!"

"Small injuries? SMALL INJURIES?! SHE ALMOST DIED, MY PLAN ALMOST KILLED HER, AND YOU WANT TO JUST WAVE THIS OFF?"

"I-I am sorry, Master, but next time... I promise it will go better!"

"I do not need you for a 'next time.'"

"No! Master! I promise that I can still be useful to you!"

"I have no interest in what you think. Go bother Orion, he is over at Brownrock Mountain. You can find your own way. There is nothing more I need from you. I must not allow myself to fail again, not like this."

Thistleman carefully picked up Diane and then began to walk back towards the city.

Sayomi turned her scathing gaze back towards the cave, tears of rage dripping down her face.

"Why couldn't you all have just died like the obedient pawns you were meant to be? Well, I can still make a small detour before going to find Orion. If I have to suffer this humiliation, then all of you... *all of you will pay for this!*"

Gungnir woke with a groan. His whole body was pain.

"Mama, one little hooman has waked," said the largest ogre.

As the female ogre lurched forward, Gungnir closed his eyes. *This is the end.*

"Hooman, why you attack us? We do no harm, we live far and in peace. Why you come and kill my children?"

The voice was full of pain and suffering. Gungnir opened his eyes, and looked into her face, and in spite of her terrible visage, he could see it racked with tears and pain.

"What? You... you kidnapped a man and brought him here to eat him."

"What you say? I tell you, we do no harm, take no people, eat no people! Why, why you attack us and hurt family?"

A sinking feeling started to overwhelm Gungnir, a terrible realization setting in. If they didn't kidnap anyone, then why did they come here?

A horrible scream, far more terrible than anything he had heard before, echoed down the hall.

All of the ogres' faces turned pale. They grabbed their clubs, axes and hammers and turn to the entrance to the hall.

"WHY? WHY YOU HUNT US?! WHAT WE DO?!" Mother Ogre yelled.

A chorus of malicious laughs echoed down the hall, followed by a creeping cold wind. The torches blew out one by one. In the flickering light of the last torch, the figure of a woman stepped out of the shadows.

"Sayomi?"

Gungnir wanted to shout at her to run but then, he saw it, the skin of an ogre being dragged in one hand, the tail and wings made of darkness behind her, blood covering her entire body and a malicious smile across her face as a maddening laugh escaping her lips.

The ogres screamed and bellowed as they charged her, as the last torch flickered out. In the darkness, all Gungnir could hear were the shrieks of the ogres. He tried to crawl away from the noise and the terror as fast as he could. Flesh was rending, blood spraying and landing on his face and body.

"Hehehehe, are you scared?"

Gungnir felt something soft press into his back and the voice sent a cold shiver down his spine.

"Now it's your turn. Where to start? I have already peeled so many skins. Maybe, lets open you up, and see how many organs I can remove, one at a time, before you die. Ehehehehe!"

A searing pain pierced his side as something entered his body—a hand, grasping, and catching hold of his kidney.

After a few more minutes, the shrieks were silenced and all that could be heard was laughter.

Epilogue:
The Little She-Devil of Njord

I groaned as I slowly opened my eyes. *Why is my vision so blurry? Everything hurts. Please tell me it didn't happen again.*

I tried to reach up to my face. The seemingly simple action felt as though it ignited a roaring fire in my arm and I cried out.

"Diane! Lay still! You are seriously hurt. Stop trying to push yourself."

Thistleman stood beside my bed, his face was creased with worry. Behind him, Emily was laid out on a hay mattress, covered in bandages.

Ryme and Jotuun were also asleep in the corner, their clothes covered in our blood, and there was a pile of bloody bandages piled next to them.

My eyes began to feel heavy again, as my labored breathing eased slightly.

Thistleman's eyes never left mine as I drifted back to sleep. Slowly he kneeled by my bed, crossed his arms, and rested his chin on them. Even though his face still showed concern, his eyes hardened, boiling with rage.

Everyone, I lost everyone.

Tears rolled down Emily's cheeks.

Why am I the only one who got to live?

Emily couldn't forget the sight of those huge, brutish creatures barreling towards her and the faces of her friends turned pale in fear.

"Still not saying anything, huh?" Thistleman said as he entered the room with a try of food. Emily tried to hide her face deeper under the covers, with only her eyes peeping slightly out.

Thistleman popped a squat right next to her as he stared unblinkingly.

What is he doing?

"If you wanna stay a mute forever, that's your business. As far as I am concerned, you are beyond useless, practically sacrificing yourself to save people who were too stupid to listen to you. If it were up to me, I would have left you to die."

Emily tried to swallow, her throat quickly turning dry. Thistleman's eyes radiated a cold, emotionless calculation, and her body trembled in response as if she was chilled to the bone.

"I am curious though, why did you do it? What about them made you willing to step into an ogre's path?"

Tears welled up in Emily's eyes and her face flushed with anger as his words wormed their way through her mind.

"Fine. Keep your silence." Thistleman stopped at the doorway, before looking back over his shoulder with a slight smile. "Just remember, Diane told me to grab you, so you pretty much owe her your life. No dying until you pay her back, or else I will make sure you suffer!"

In her silence, Emily had found a new pastime to occupy her, and that was loathing Thistleman. For now, at the very least, she had forgotten some of the despair which had been plaguing her.

As Diane recovered, she began to go on quests again and, soon, she was starting to hone and master her skills. Every day she would read through her book. In it, she could feel immeasurable knowledge and power.

"Is she back again from another quest? Goodness me! She is covered with blood."

"What did she kill this time? I heard she went after a small goblin raiding party…"

"Look out, she is coming through! It's that bloody girl. What is her problem? She's got this wild, obsessive look on her face."

"Another quest? Again? Doesn't she take a break?"

"Why does that boy keep following that monster girl around. Do you think he's like her too?"

"This is new. Looks like she is dragging another girl along with her."

"There they go again. That poor girl looks so scared next to that little devil! And yet they are always traveling around together. I hope nothing happens to her."

Emily was taking a bath when her relaxation was interrupted by a capricious laugh.

"Teeehehehe, Emmmmm! Oh dear Eeemmmily! I need your help, Big Sis!"

Emily's eyes affixed themselves in terror to the door of the bathroom. She promptly pulled her hat lower and tried to sink deeper into the water, as a feeling of dread permeated her bones.

Footsteps echoed down the hall....

After what felt like an eternity, the shadow passed the doorframe as Diane's calls grew distant again. After a minute of silence, Emily breathed a sigh of relief.

Click.

The window above her bath flew open. Emily shrieked, certainly not for the last time.

That was the first time Diane 'abducted' Emily for training. From there, it only got more demanding, as Emily rapidly learned the terror of an ten year old child with a tad too much power...

And at first, as much as she wanted to, she couldn't get herself to speak a single word of complaint.

She got abducted:

When she was eating.

When she was shopping.

On a nice, quiet date.

Going for a walk.

Getting abducted by bandits... just to get abducted by Diane again.

Days blended into weeks, and the weeks blended into months, through winter and into spring. No less than once a week, Diane would return from a quest covered in some creature or other's blood. Several times a week she would she drag Emily on a quest with her and Thistleman.

Not that Emily could go anywhere even if she wanted to. The few times she tried to sneak out, Thistleman and Clover always happened to wander in to block the doorway. She couldn't handle his cold stare. Then there was Diane, she had a supernatural sense for finding her any time she had managed to get alone time outside.

Lastly, there was Rhyme and Jotuun. How such sweet creatures as them wound up sheltering those two, she could not figure out. But at least they made her food, and tended to her nicely and didn't take advantage of her silence.

People also began to take notice that the orphaned children that once roamed the streets were slowly disappearing, even as the war to the west raged on and families were destroyed. Soon, stories of Diane began to circulate as though she was the boogeyman.

"Listen to me good here, Bjorn! I know you have seen that little she-devil running around here, always coming back late at night and covered in blood. Do you know where she gets it from? Well I'll tell ya, it's from all the bad boys who don't listen to their mothers! If you don't start behaving, she will abduct you like those orphans and you will be just another blood splotch on her skirt!"

Around this time, there were also unconfirmed sightings of another little girl carrying an oversized scythe. Apparently, she stood on the rooftops of the buildings around the slums late at night. However, just as quickly as she was seen, she disappeared.

Soon, Diane's new nickname spread across the kingdom. Tales of the Little She-Devil of Njord could no longer be suppressed. Tales that would bring the attention of many new eyes to the former Viking town.

The Year of Emperor Hirihito IV: 240
Mist Vale, Kingdom of Luthas

"You must not forget... you must never forget"

Amala tossed and turned restlessly in bed, her mind plagued by a vision she first had more than a month ago.

"Spare her life and send her north. More than just your freedom will depend on it."

Amala shot up from her bed, her breathing wild and a cold sweat dousing her body and her sheets. She let out a small groan.

These damned nightmares. I should have never stopped to pray at Almalexia's temple. The priest even said they hadn't felt her inspiration in months, and now I appear to be cursed.

Her small room at the inn felt very constricting for a moment, but she was soon able to regain control of her breathing. At least the people here were surprisingly welcoming. She had been worried that the people here might be suspicious of her as an outsider, but as she spoke with the innkeeper and told them her story, their expressions changed from tense to relief. Even the other people in the town would smile and wave at her.

They were quite the pleasant elderly couple, I still can't believe they let me get this room for free!

Amala allowed herself a smile as she looked out the darkened window, enjoying the sight of a nice fog bank rolling in over the town.

Shortly after the fog rolled in, Amala heard a soft knock at the door.

"Dearie, are you alright? May we come in?"

"Yes you may, it is quite alright."

As the door swung open, all the hair on Amala's arm stood on end, and her skin was covered in goosebumps.

Next to the little old innkeeper stood an extremely tall and thin old man, wearing a trench coat and dark leather clothing. He was wearing a bowler hat, which somehow felt like it contrasted his gaunt, pale face and cold, lifeless eyes.

"Ah, my Lady Amala, since I heard of your arrival in my small, quiet town, I have been... hungering to make your acquaintance. My name is Mobius, Mobius Strathclyde."

Mobius strode across the room towards Amala's bed. Her eyes went wide in fear. She was unable to open her mouth to let out a single sound. Her body trembled, but with a moment's push with all of her will, she broke the gaze of Mobius and sprinted to the window... and then froze before attempting to leap out.

They're all, every last one, in on it.

The entire town was standing around the inn, all of them with peaceful smiles plastered on their faces. All of them watching Amala's window—the friendly shopkeeper who gave her an extra apple; the stable master who recommended the inn, and the craftsman who offered to clean and sharpen her sword for free.

"Now now, Lady Amala, where did you think you were trying to run off to? I really hate it when I have to give chase."

This is it, then. All or nothing.

Amala reached into her pajamas and pulled out a hidden dagger, swiftly twisting around with a strike to Mobius' throat... when she met his gaze again. Her body froze in place, unable to move.

"Ahhhh, but I do enjoy the feisty ones. I can make good use of you, even after I take my fill and dine."

Amala felt a sharp pain in her neck, unable to move, unable to scream, her face frozen in pain and the surreal feeling of this silent, smiling town watching her... somehow, she kept remembering her dream.

Milton Keynes UK
Ingram Content Group UK Ltd.
UKHW052247280524
443311UK00008B/188